Lies of War

Lies of War

a novel

Laurence Gadd

The North River Press Publishing Corporation
P.O. Box 567
Great Barrington, MA 01230
www.northriverpress.com

ISBN: 978-088427-2083

For information or rights contact:
The North River Press
P.O. Box 567, Great Barrington, MA 01230
www.northriverpress.com

For CIA

Acknowledgments

My appreciation to those people and institutions who helped and supported me during the years spent working and avoiding working on this book.

The Imperial War Museum captured my attention in the 1960s and continued to transfix me during my many visits over the ensuing years. The Churchill War Rooms, which I had the opportunity to visit in their still dusty untouched state well before they were turned into a museum and became available to the public.

To my family members who tolerated me and gave great advice, some of which I took and some of which I should have taken, on the characters and how I should proceed.

To Amy at The North River Press who turned the manuscript into a book.

Most of all to Rachel and Cia, who read, advised, researched, edited and reread, advised, researched, and edited innumerable times and never gave up.

Lies of War

PART I

There was a small damp stain on the front of his uniform trousers, he couldn't take a deep breath without experiencing agonizing pain just above his pubic area, and he could feel his heart was beating rapidly under his uniform jacket. He knew he was being watched and thus remained standing as still and erect as possible. The room he was in was very ordinary; the dank smell reminded him of his clerk's office back in Berlin. To his right were two old oak desks covered with yellowing newspapers and behind him was a mismatched collection of wooden office chairs.

The opposite wall was false, although he did not know that, and behind it were two large windows. All he could see was the false wall that had been painted in military tan and the mirror through which he was being watched. The prisoner, although exhausted from his flight and detainment, remained ramrod stiff in the middle of the room facing the door.

"Arrogant son of a bitch, isn't he?" whispered one of the two spotters being used to record Rudolph Hess' every action. "He must be ready to soil his pants by now. The bastard."

Both men had just relieved the prior spotters and would be relieved themselves in another two hours. No chance was being taken that boredom would cause some seemingly insignificant gesture to be missed. Being cramped between the windows and the false wall was not the best duty, but they both knew from personal experience that it was far better than being abroad behind enemy lines. The duty schedule was two hours watching and recording, one hour debriefing, which was more like an inquisition, and five hours off. There were four teams of two each and one team in reserve. In another, not much better furnished room across the hall from Hess, the debriefing of Evans and Cornith was just beginning.

"First I want your general impressions. Is he tired? Afraid? Or angry? Is there anything about him that seems different from this morning? You know the drill—even the smallest mannerism can give us a clue to his real purpose for being here."

"The thing I can't understand is that he has been here almost twelve hours and not asked for the loo. I would be pounding on the door by now or just using a corner of the room." Evans was a contradiction, he was pale and small and seemingly shy, almost effeminate in appearance, but as any member of the team knew, he was perfectly capable of pulling his car over and using church steps, if the urge arose, to relieve himself. Dr. Kornrich interrupted him in a booming voice.

"We all know your disgusting habits, Ian, but you must understand some of us have control over our bowels. The pressure on his bladder and the urge to defecate is soon going to cause Hess to react in some way. He will be compelled, as you say, to use the corner of the room and suffer the indignity of behaving in an uncivilized manner, or he will be forced to ask for our permission to use the toilet. Either way his steel will be weakened and he will begin to view himself as a prisoner and not the Teutonic tower of strength he now pretends to be."

"Kirkpatrick is already on his way from London and it would be very helpful if we had already placed Herr Hess in a state of agitation."

"It should be Herr Kirkpatrick. The bastard's as much a Nazi as the martinet in the next room," added Roger Cornith. "That fine example of British civil servant has spent more time rubbing bellies with the wives and sons of the Third Reich than gathering intelligence. You should read some of the reports from the former first secretary of our embassy in Berlin. If I had put mine where his has been, I'd have it cut off."

"Enough. This is a debriefing, not a military tribunal of the civil service, even if you two think that would be justified. How is he reacting? How long do you think he can hold on? Ian, what's your best guess?"

"Not much longer. I would think one more watch at the most. You agree, Roger?"

"Exactly correct. How long before Kirkpatrick gets here, Doctor?"

"About three hours. We are going to apply some more pressure by disrupting his concentration. I want a bell to ring at random times but never in intervals shorter than fifteen minutes. This should rattle him some. Now you two get some rest. If we progress as you think, I will want you alert, as you may be needed."

Dr. Kornrich was always amazed at how much time could be wasted by university educated, well-trained military intelligence personnel at briefings. He understood their display of disdain for anyone belonging to some other club. In time of war the other club was often replaced by branch of service, or, as in this case, by the civil service. Kornrich was a British subject, although his sense of belonging was thousands of miles away. He had been born almost seventy years earlier in Quebec City and although deeply engrossed in his work for the British government he missed that beautiful city and his office on a hill overlooking the St. Lawrence River. His vast experience treating psychotic patients in both Canada and the United States, and his record as a medical officer during the last war, had made him the logical choice to head up interrogator training for military intelligence. Kornrich had not yet fully examined his own feelings about the intentional creation of psychosis in prisoners. There was no question that a prisoner, when pushed to a point of total exhaustion and agitation, would be less in control and therefore reveal weaknesses that could be used to break him down during interrogation. But what was his obligation to these men after the interrogators were finished with them? Could these broken men be sent to the harsh environment of prisoner of war camps as cowards and traitors and face those who had not been broken? It would be as if he had killed them himself.

WASHINGTON, DC
SEPTEMBER 12, 1941

At a side entrance to Washington's Union Station Morris Gold was met by Undersecretary of State Sumner Welles and his aide, Major Robert Blackstone. Gold, in his typically rumpled three-piece suit, climbed into the back seat of the black Packard, quickly sliding behind the driver so that his deaf left ear would be at the window and he could hear the other passengers with his good ear. Over the years this maneuver had become so automatic that he rarely realized he was doing it. The hearing loss had been caused by a severe childhood infection that had almost cost him his life, but had had little effect on him as an adult short of keeping him from going overseas in 1917 or applying for a driver's license. Gold felt that his inability to distinguish the direction a sound was coming from would be hazardous to other drivers, and living in New York with its abundance of busses, els, and hacks made an automobile unnecessary.

Washington was at its best. The oppressive heat of the summer had finally broken and it was cool enough to keep the car, with its windows closed, relatively comfortable.

Not a word was spoken until they had dropped the major off outside Hecht's department store on F

Street. His impression was that the need for Major Blackstone's presence had been to identify him, but Gold had no recollection of ever having met Blackstone. The car quickly pulled up to an alley leading to the rear entrance of the Mayflower Hotel.

"Mr. Gold, the rear elevator is waiting for you. Please take it to suite 776 and hand the men at the door this card. My driver will be waiting for you in the lobby and drive you back to the station."

Gold did exactly as he was told. He was no stranger to Washington or to the machinations of over-tedious security personnel. It was always best not to question unimportant indignities.

"It's good to see you again, Mr. Gold. The president is waiting for you in the bedroom. It looks like you're having a private session."

Morris always wondered if this Secret Service agent, who looked about forty pounds overweight, could really protect the man on crutches without crushing him.

"Thank you, Tom," Gold said with a smile. "I can see that life is treating you well. Sorry I don't have a package from Barney Greengrass for you."

Greengrass was the New York delicatessen that made shipments of sturgeon, Scotch salmon, and smoked whitefish to the president for Sunday breakfasts. It was Tom Quinn's job to pick up and inspect the package every week, and it was common White House knowledge that Quinn could not resist "tasting the food for the president's protection."

President Roosevelt was sitting up in bed, his legs propped up on a pillow, fully dressed except for his jacket. The lights were all on, and the room, except for the president on the bed, looked perfectly made up and unoccupied. Gold could see from his old friend's appearance that whatever this meeting was about, it had the president worried.

"Morris, you and I, Tom outside, and the secretary of war are the only ones who know of this meeting. Even poor Sumner doesn't know who you are meeting. He must be angry as hell at being used as an errand boy by the secretary. He is certainly not accustomed to such treatment. It might do him a little good, although that's unlikely.

"Morris, we have a problem of such magnitude that the very survival of our Christian world may depend on us finding a solution, so don't interrupt me with any questions until I finish. Rudolf Hess, as you know, parachuted into Scotland four months ago with a peace plan. What you don't know is that he has revealed enough other information for us to believe that Germany is within two years of developing a weapon so powerful that one bomb could completely destroy the city of London. If we are to believe the best estimates of our scientists, Hess' new information shows us to be at least two years behind Germany.

"Mo," the president said, using Morris' childhood nickname, "we have to interrupt Germany's progress and gain access to their research. I need you to take charge of this. You and very few others must be the only ones to know what the true situation is. Even Winston believes that we are much further along than we actually are. No one else must know. I don't think I have to explain in detail why I have chosen you, but part of the reason is that, although we go back a long time, few people are aware of the extent of our relationship, your close friendship with Jimmy, or the time spent with us at Hyde Park. You are the person I can trust with this. I have briefed Willie Sherman and instructed him to give you every assistance possible. Class of twenty-one. Do you remember him? Well, he remembers you. In any event Willie is familiar with the situation in London and can help you get what you need in Washington without causing an uproar. You know how important I feel it is to defeat Nazis, but with this weapon in Hitler's hands I fear the war could be over before I can get us in there. Winston is a tough bird, but if he knew the true status of our research even he would lose some of his wind. Mo, you have to move fast and you can't make any mistakes. All of us are depending on you."

"Franklin—Mr. President, I know you don't scare easily, but aren't you grossly overstating the power of this bomb? London has millions of inhabitants. I will, of course, do as you ask, but I certainly don't need an exaggerated perspective to work from. I'm sure no single bomb could—"

"I am not exaggerating. Mo, you have to trust that I had the same doubts you're expressing when I returned from my Placentia Bay meeting with Winston, but I am convinced. Although I don't fully understand the process, the potential results were explained to me in terrifying detail. Whoever develops this bomb first will have a death grip on their enemies."

"I will need some form of authorization."

"I will prepare an executive order under the War Powers Act and sign it the day we declare war on Germany. Until then you will have to work through Willie Sherman. Any other authorization would raise questions in Congress, something we cannot afford. This order, once issued, will give you more power than any man on earth. Even I have to answer to the people and to Congress. You won't."

After dismissing his driver in the lobby, Gold walked the short distance to the Hay-Adams hotel, his favorite, checked in, and took a taxi to the Colonial Bar in Georgetown for a drink and time to reflect on the day's events. The Colonial was a standard hangout for Washington personalities. It was decorated to resemble an early American tavern and, in fact, most of the furnishings were as authentic as anything at Mt. Vernon. As they approached Georgetown, Gold could almost smell the wood and leather and the history that permeated the Colonial.

All this faded when he got out of the taxi and saw Major Blackstone pulling up alongside the curb in a black Packard much like the one that had taken him to see the president. Blackstone took Gold by the arm and with authority, but not forcefully, escorted him to the Packard.

"I'm sorry to grab you off the street like that, but after you dismissed your driver I had a hell of a time finding you. It's a good thing I got to see you at the station as I would never have recognized you from these old photographs."

Blackstone was holding pictures of Gold's Harvard Law School graduation twenty years earlier. With the age difference and the old-fashioned stiff collar it was, in fact, difficult to recognize him. The most identifiable thing about the picture was that although the young Gold was posing in his finest suit on a personally momentous occasion, he looked decidedly rumpled.

"Colonel Sherman sends his greetings and has instructed me to escort you to him."

"I am afraid, Major, that we will have to disappoint 'Wild Willie' as I am going to go in the Colonial, have a whiskey, and then go back to the Hay-Adams for a good night's sleep. If you will call for me promptly at eight tomorrow morning, I will be happy to meet with the colonel. Good night, Major."

Gold walked away from the car and through the entrance to the Colonial.

WASHINGTON, D.C.
SEPTEMBER 13, 1941

Morris Gold did not get a good night's sleep. Instead
he spent most of the night trying to work out some
preliminary approach to the problem. He knew that
any chance for success was based on his taking full
responsibility right from the start. There could be no
doubt about the lines of authority. His encounter with
Blackstone was the first in what he was sure would be
many attempts to limit his power. His meeting with
Sherman the next morning would have to be tough.
The president had given him the authority and the
responsibility, and if he had to be unpleasant in exer-
cising it, so be it. Gold also knew that an unsigned
presidential order was not enough. Franklin would
have to do better. Gold had to have a legal document
that could survive both Franklin Roosevelt and Morris Gold, a document that would protect not only himself and his family, but the future of American Jews.
If the information was wrong about German progress
on this bomb, or if his actions were somehow exposed,
Gold could not be sure that his old friend in the White
House, if still alive, would be willing to stand by him.
He did not want to leave any chance of his failure being
used as an excuse to attack the loyalty of American

Jews. What was happening in Germany could happen in the United States and Gold knew of many people in positions of power who would support it. In addition to what he had offered, Gold would insist on a personal letter in the president's own handwriting taking full responsibility for Gold's actions, naming him special counsel to the president to ensure the privileged nature of their relationship, and protecting him with a blanket presidential pardon. This paper would have to be witnessed by two individuals, one of the president's choosing and one of his own. Gold knew he would use Eleanor as his witness and wondered who was left for her husband to choose.

The telephone rang at 7:15.

"Good morning, Mr. Gold, this is the front desk. Your car is waiting."

He was not surprised by this early arrival. Willie Sherman was an in-fighter, and in Washington intimidation was the blue plate special. Gold had been awake for an hour and was just finishing his coffee, his first cigarette of the day, and the late city edition of the *New York Times*. The same breakfast he would have had at home, or anywhere the *Times* could be delivered.

"Please tell the driver I will be downstairs at eight o'clock." As he uncapped his fountain pen he thought: "Forty-five minutes, more than enough time to complete the crossword."

The tall man in his rumpled suit impressed Sherman. Not many men stood up to him with such grace.

13

Since his arrival he had noted that Gold was both charming and direct. Not what he expected. More like a Jesuit than a Jew. The two men quickly agreed on their respect for the cheesecake at Lindy's, Packard automobiles, and the President of the United States. They also agreed to their disdain for Stalin, Joseph Kennedy, the Department of War, the Democrats, the Republicans, and most of the Washington political establishment. Both felt it was a good enough beginning to use their given names.

Sherman did not seem able to sit still. To Morris he appeared as a gentleman ice skater; he was literally gliding around the room, from the windows overlooking the Capitol building, down one side of the oversized antique desk, around Morris sitting in the side chair, and back to the window. Perfect figure eights. When he finally slid into the other side chair he crossed his legs as if ready to remove his skates. It was time to get down to business.

Morris spoke first. "Our first task is to determine the possibility of such a weapon. It is beyond my scope of knowledge and my very comprehension that such a destructive power can be created by man. All wars cost lives, but one bomb able to annihilate the population of an entire town?"

"Morris, Einstein was emphatic. It can be done."

"I thought he might find an exception to his deeply held anti-war beliefs, although philosophically against all war he would come to believe that we must use all means to stop Hitler. What better way to pressure FDR than to forecast such a development? And I'm not sure the president believes him either."

"The president may or may not believe him, but we have been charged with that determination, and physics or chemistry or whatever is involved here is not my forte."

"What is involved is war of a greater magnitude, something we can both understand. The possibility of thousands of bombs, each able to destroy an entire town."

"Morris. Cities, not towns."

"I understand." Morris realized that even in his disbelief, he wished to minimize the implications of this weapon. He began to understand why the president of the United States had chosen Morris Gold, forty-three years old, born Moshe Goldstein, son of an immigrant tailor. It was his ability to move in any circle without being an insider. More precisely it was his inability to become an insider. It was being a Jew, Harvard Law Review, a clerkship with Justice Brandeis, coauthor of the definitive antitrust text, respected for his intellect and rejected for his heritage. But he knew the difference between an aromatic seeded rye bread and a soft dinner roll, he believed in the ethical foundation of his faith and often wondered if that foundation was not a result of the acerbity of the god of the Jews. How much easier to cross the line if your god is kindly and forgiving. For Morris, ethical behavior was a given, not from fear of a vindictive god, rather from a presence, as ingrained as his genetic makeup. Passed parent to child. Undiluted from immigrant father to American son.

Sherman interrupted Gold's private thoughts. "Before we move on to the matter of Herr Hess, for obvious reasons I suggest that you make a stop on your return to New York and meet with Professor Einstein."

"Ah, a little Jew to Jew chat," Morris thought, noting Sherman's emphasis on the word you.

"An excellent suggestion, Willie, I think that would be quite appropriate."

"Good. Now, have you had the opportunity to read this most confusing report from London?"

"Yes, your young man was kind enough to avail me of it while I was waiting in your anteroom."

"I do apologize, Morris, Washington habits are hard to break. It won't happen again."

"Thank you. I do agree about the report. Lord Simon believes Hess, Kirkpatrick isn't sure, and former ambassador Kennedy thinks it shouldn't matter to us. Then there is that odd addendum by the Canadian doctor."

"The British are taking it quite seriously. They have conducted extensive bombing raids of the research center in Brest, five times in May alone, and have established some research program of their own called 'tube alloys'. Maybe you'll be able to clarify the science with Einstein, something about sustained reactions and uranium isotopes. All beyond me."

"We have an anxious president. When he met Churchill in Newfoundland last month he agreed to advise the prime minister of our progress, if any, on developing our own bomb. Apparently he had to confess to relative ignorance of the subject. FDR without an opinion, I'm sure that wasn't a comfortable moment for him.

"You know, Einstein did warn him about this in thirty-nine. He wrote suggesting he find someone trustworthy but not in the public eye to explore this."

"I guess you are the chosen one," Sherman said with a smile. "Appropriate, don't you think?"

LAURENCE GADD

PRINCETON, NEW JERSEY
SEPTEMBER 14, 1941

On the train to Princeton, Gold tried to organize his thoughts. He had come a long way from Perry Street in Greenwich Village, when he used to steal rides on the back of a milk wagon. He was going to meet with the world's greatest scientist, the Galileo of the twentieth century, he was a confidant of the president of the United States, and was about to be instrumental in trying to save "the Christian world" from fascism. He laughed to himself. A most appropriate path for one of the chosen people.

"Mr. Gold, it is my pleasure to meet the president's representative and I must thank you again for your assistance in my little exodus. My little boat. We will sail around in circles. You will join me? Anna has prepared a luncheon for us. Pot roasted sandwiches I believe. I hope you will enjoy them."

Albert Einstein was dressed in tan trousers, canvas shoes, and a blue shirt of a style Gold had never seen. It was either some old country sailing garment or what remained of his nightshirt. Einstein handed him a picnic basket and led him to the door.

"Good, we will talk on the lake. I will sail and you will listen. Yes?"

Gold realized that the questions did not require

18

answers, and that Morris Gold and Albert Einstein were about to go sailing.

Although Morris knew nothing of sailing, he did know that his captain was not paying very much attention to where he was going. Whereas Sherman skated perfect figure eights, Einstein's circles consisted of sailing until you almost hit something and then abruptly turning. But diagrams were drawn in water and on the boat's floorboards, and the explanations of splitting the atom, self-sustaining chain reactions, and the need for a substance called heavy water, although interrupted by frequent near calamities, were cogent enough for Gold to understand. In the middle of the lake Einstein let the sail loose and the boat drifted.

"Do you know that when I wrote to the president in nineteen-thirty-nine, I warned him of the possibilities. Now it is more than a possibility, it is a major possibility, no, it is quite likely. I determine this not from your disheartening news, but on the probability of progress beyond that already achieved when I last was able to correspond with my former colleagues. But now I must think if it is true. If a self-sustaining chain reaction has been achieved, I calculate that, if all available resources are applied, and the sun chooses to shine on us, it will take three years to achieve equal to the German progress as we are minimum one year from them. With ideal conditions, no wrong paths, no major miscalculations, they are possibly two years from completion with a greater than fifty percent probability it will be accomplished in three years."

Gold said nothing. He was trying to recast Einstein's last statement; to restate it in his mind so he understood. The Germans could possibly have an atom bomb in two years, and can probably have one in three years. It will take us at least three years to develop our own bomb, and then only if we apply extraordinary efforts and are very lucky.

RAF HORNCHURCH AIRFIELD
ESSEX, ENGLAND
OCTOBER 13, 1941

Gold, in the uniform of an American colonel, jumped down from the hatch, stumbled, and fell.

"I'm getting too old for this," he thought, dusting himself off. The flights had taken eighteen hours and that did not include the ten-hour train trip from New York to Montreal, or the two-and-a-half-hour drive to the airfield. Gold was exhausted. Already half deaf, he now could barely hear in his one good ear.

The Canadian ferry pilots, both young women, could not be in much better shape. After three stops to refuel, their final landing included several bone jarring bounces. It seemed a miracle the wheels had not collapsed.

At the end of the field he could see what appeared to be a small open car throwing up voluminous dust as it approached. His heart sank, realizing this was to be his transportation.

"Colonel Davidson? Welcome to England, sir. Pleasant journey I trust?"

Her eyes were enough. She wore a military coat, and a scarf that covered her head and most of her face. As the dust settled Gold focused on the intense but humorous look he was receiving.

"Eh, yes, it was fine, thank you. Let me just get my valise from the airplane."

"My responsibility, sir. If you will just have a seat I will only be a moment." She reached across, opened the passenger side door and leapt from the car in one continuous movement. Before Gold could say a word, she was back with his luggage.

"Do get in," she said with a smile. "We must clear the field."

"Who manufactured this car?" Gold asked as they sped away.

"It's a thirty-seven Bentley 4.25 liter with a blower, really quite fast. It belongs to my father, but since I am serving it is mine to use. He has a driver now anyway and I believe he feels undignified in a drophead. Do you like dropheads?"

Gold had no idea what she was talking about.

"Oh, lord, here I am blathering on and I haven't introduced myself. Mary Wainwright of His Majesty's Service, at your disposal, sir."

"Well, Miss Wainwright of His Majesty's Service, I have one very important question for you."

"Sir?"

"What is a drophead?"

During the ride Gold learned that Mary Wainwright was the daughter of Air Vice-Marshal George Forrest-Wainwright (currently military liaison to the American embassy), had a first from Cambridge in literature, was not married but had almost been twice, drove very fast and, of course, that a drophead coupe was a convertible. It all made sense to Gold; anything this remarkable woman said made sense to him.

"My instructions are to drop you at your embassy, but if you want to freshen up first I can take you to your billet, and wait. You're staying at Browns. I hope that's satisfactory, I find it rather silly and much prefer the Connaught. You seem to be quite the important visitor. Last month General Smith was put up at the Viceroy on Knightsbridge Road, definably a step down. The bar at the Connaught is simply splendid and it would have been far more convenient. But Lincoln Bradley, the ambassador's aide, made the reservation, so Browns it will be."

Gold was struggling to hear her every word. If this had been New York he would have been on the wrong side of the car and able to hear almost nothing.

Without thinking he said, "Take me there, to the Connaught."

"There I am going on again, you must think me some chatty schoolgirl, or worse. Of course you should go to Browns, it's a very nice hotel. All you Americans want to stay there, it is very old English, quite the experience."

"No, I know a good suggestion when I hear one. The Connaught will suit me just fine."

"Marvelous, I will have you there in twenty minutes."

"Then will you have a whiskey with me at that splendid bar of yours? I need to be revived after this trip."

"I am so very sorry, everyone thinks I drive too fast, and with the roof down too. I am sorry, it must be awful for you. I'm such a scatter sometimes."

"No, you're wonderful—I mean this trip is wonderful. No, not that, your driving—I mean it's—oh hell, I think your driving is terrific."

With that said Gold promptly fell asleep, leaving Mary to consider this middle-aged Yank snoring in the seat beside her.

After Gold bathed and changed into civilian clothes he found Mary in the bar protecting a chair for him.

"Here you are," she said, touching his arm. "I told them an American officer was joining me or I wouldn't have gotten the table. Now I imagine they think I was fibbing. You look wrinkled enough to be a barrister."

"I'm afraid I have already given my uniform for pressing, otherwise I would certainly go back and change."

"You wouldn't."

"No, I wouldn't, not after you disobeyed orders and dragged me to the Connaught. This place is wonderful. You won't get into trouble, will you?"

"No, I rang up the embassy and told them you had a change in plans. Totally out of my control you see."

Gold caught his breath. There was that smile and those crinkled brown eyes again. He thought she was beautiful, but he had thought that from the moment he had first seen her. Now he was studying her. Brown hair pinned up, exposing her long perfect neck, a perfect face, perfect ears, in fact everything he saw seemed perfect. He dwelled in the moment.

"You're staring at me, say something before I turn a hideous color red."

Signaling, Gold said, "I need a whiskey, and you?"

"Yes, of course," and turning to the waiter, she ordered. "A whiskey for my colonel here and one for myself as well please."

"Really, if you're going to have a trouble about the switch in hotels I'm sure I can fix it."

"No, when I rang up the embassy I spoke to Daddy. He'll make things right."

What Mary Wainwright did not say was that she had also rung up her control officer at MI5, British military intelligence.

CONNAUGHT HOTEL
LONDON
OCTOBER 14, 1941

The next morning it didn't matter to Gold that he awoke to the sound of rain on his window. He had slept well and had only the faintest memory of a dream about his father fitting a tweed suit on Mary Wainwright somewhere on a beach in Spain with shells exploding all around them. It had not been a nightmare or even a bad dream and it was fading quickly as he thought of the upcoming day. Mary was to pick him up outside the hotel, drive him to the embassy, and wait while he paid his respects, as it were, to the ambassador.

Gold had never met the ambassador. He had however met his predecessor, Joseph Kennedy, twice. First at a dinner for the president and then at a party given by Al Smith. Gold knew from these two meetings that Kennedy was Ambassador to the Court of St. James only because he had contributed a huge sum to FDR's campaign chest, and that if the United States came close to entering the war he would be replaced. Kennedy was a staunch advocate of staying out of the war, admired Hitler, and had a distinct distaste for Jews. Morris Gold did not like the man and wondered how different his replacement could be. He was not looking forward to this meeting. But being a man who believed in starting the day out right, he poured himself a cup of coffee, lit a cigarette, uncapped his pen, and opened the *London Times* to its crossword page.

Mary was sitting in the lobby reading that paper. As she stood, he thought, "I must get a grip on myself and concentrate on why I'm here. I'm acting like a schoolboy."

"Good morning, Miss Wainwright," he said formally.

"Yes, of course, good morning. Are your rooms pleasant enough?"

"Yes, I think so. I fell asleep so quickly I barely had time to look around, and this morning the crossword was totally engrossing." In fact, it remained unfinished on his nightstand.

"I'm so relieved. I brought a copy of the *Times* for you and then just couldn't resist and solved the crossword while I was waiting for you."

Gold sighed, knowing it was hopeless. Her car, a large black limousine, was parked directly in front of the hotel.

"Well, this is certainly not a drophead," Gold said, exhibiting his new automotive knowledge.

"Very good, Colonel, no, this is a Daimler. When I explained to the motor pool how important a visitor you were, they issued me the best they had. Of course if I didn't have such an important motorcar I would have had to stay with it and wait on the mews, not in front. The Connaught has its rules, you know."

"I'm learning."

When she opened the rear passenger door, Gold climbed in, deciding that he could use a few feet of separation from this young woman.

The streets of London were filled with double-tiered buses, much like the number fives on Riverside Drive, taxis quite unlike the DeSoto Skyviews of New York, a great variety of trucks and, of course, bicycles with riders of every description. But Gold was not paying attention. His mind was focused on his upcoming meeting.

"Have you met the ambassador?" he called to the front seat.

"Oh no. Of course I did meet ambassador Kennedy several times, he brought his family to Checkers once, and at embassy events. His children seem right enough."

"Do I understand a disapproval of the former ambassador?"

"Perhaps you should have this conversation with someone of authority. Shall I wait for you at the embassy?"

"Please, I won't be very long and I have another appointment. Do you know where Wormwood Scrubs Prison is?"

"Oh my, no."

"Is there a discreet way for you to find out?"

"Of course, I understand."

The car pulled up to the embassy and Mary was holding his door open before he could even think about opening it himself. "How does she manage to do that?" he wondered.

"I shouldn't be very long, a half hour at the most."

"Right, sir," she said, giving him a salute.

After being told that the ambassador was in conference, a butler walked past headed for the inner office. Gold observed a coffee pot and only one cup and saucer on his tray. Gold turned to the ambassador's secretary and said, "It looks like the ambassador is conferring with himself."

When he walked out of the embassy five minutes later he had not seen the ambassador but had already decided that he must do something about this Mary Wainwright. The car was waiting for him. This time, without thinking, he moved quickly and was in the front seat beside her before she even knew he was there.

"Do we know where we are going?" he asked.

"You surprised me. Yes, it's off to Elephant and Castle. I'm afraid there may be some bomb damage and we may have to detour around a bit. What time is your appointment?"

"I don't think it matters when we arrive. Unlike the ambassador, I'm quite sure he will have the time to see me."

"Oh dear, is the colonel having a trying morning?" she said, smiling at him.

"My dear young lady, I think we should clarify something right now. I cannot be distracted. I believe you were selected as my driver because of your connections to the embassy, and that, although you know no details, you are aware of the serious nature of my mission. Please drive on."

The trip through London, although punctuated by the chilled lack of conversation, was an education for Gold. Whole blocks were bombed flat, sometimes only a single building would remain and other times only one building would be in ruins as if knocked over on a chess board. They did indeed have to make several detours around rubble-strewn streets, but in time they arrived at Wormwood Scrubs Prison. The entrance was a small, gated door halfway down a narrow street of windowless wall.

Mary deftly pulled the Daimler's two left wheels onto the sidewalk, allowing adequate room for others to pass, and turned off the engine.

Gold squeezed out, trying not to damage the car door against the brick wall Mary had parked close to.

"I don't know how long this will take. Can you wait for me here?"

"Very well, sir," was the icy reply.

As he approached the riveted black iron door he saw the sign:
RING FOR ACCESS
POSITIVELY NO ADMITTANCE.

"Only the English," Gold thought. "Why ring if you can't go in?"

Mary waited to see Gold ring and be admitted to

the prison before driving off.

"Colonel Davidson, a pleasure. If you will follow me, sir, I will just have you sign the visitors' book and then you may see the prisoner. Please do not have any physical contact with three-two-aught-one, not even in greeting him. You must stay across the table from him and not block the view of the metal mirror which you will find to your left. Now a quick inspection of your clothing and everything can move right along." After a quite thorough search, Gold was quickly led up three long double flights of stone stairs to a well-lit hallway with two wooden doors on either side and an iron door at the far end.

"Best defense strategy," his escort said, not the slightest bit out of breath. "Only one way in and the same way out. Each stair landing is a perfect defensive point with a cross field of fire. Just in case our three-two-aught-one's friends have any clever ideas of rescue or assassination. Now, do mind my instructions."

As Gold walked to the end of the hall the iron door swung toward him. He entered a small windowless room no larger than a closet. The door swung closed behind him and he could hear the latch engage. Within a moment he felt the floor seem to move under him. He grabbed the wall to steady himself and realized he was in an elevator that seemed to be moving up, then suddenly reversing direction and moving down at a far more rapid rate, then slowing and almost coming to a stop before rising again, and finally stopping.

There was no way to discern if he had come to rest on a higher or lower floor, or even the same floor as he had started from.

"A very clever, if disconcerting, technique," Gold thought. He would have to tell Willie Sherman about its effectiveness.

There were two knocks on the wall behind him and a panel swung open. The same escort greeted him without a trace of recognition.

"Follow me, sir," was all he said as he turned and quickly stepped down a long hall with Gold and two additional guards falling in behind. The four came to an abrupt halt on the right side of the hallway in front of a door with a large iron bolt. It seemed a relic of the time of dungeons. The escort slid open the peephole and called into the room.

"Move to the rear wall. Now!" This was clearly a command to be followed. The door was unbolted and Gold was maneuvered, if not pushed, to the front as it was opened. There, standing against the far wall glaring at him, was Rudolf Hess, dressed in a loose fitting gray prison uniform with no belt or tie. His shoes were without laces and he wore a brown, emblemless military jacket. Gold immediately focused on Hess' dark eyes and heavy black eyebrows, far from the Aryan image one would expect of the deputy führer of the Third Reich, but then again Hitler was no blond seductress himself.

The room was windowless and bare except for a

table with two chairs, and a cot, all bolted to the floor. From the doorway behind Gold the order "Sit" was barked. Hess moved forward slowly in a shuffling manner and stopped. He remained standing, gripping the top of one of the chairs with both hands. Again the bark, "Sit."

Gold turned to the voice and started to object when Hess abruptly moved in front of him, clicked his heels soundlessly, and said in German, "You are American, are you not?"

The escorts became apoplectic. Pushing past Gold, they grabbed Hess on both sides, lifted him, and pushed him into a chair. Because the bolted furniture could not move, Hess' violent contact with it must have been both bruising and painful.

Using the German of his paternal grandmother's kitchen, Gold replied, "Yes, my name is Colonel Davidson of the United States Army Judge Advocate General's Office. May I sit?"

"Yes, of course, the deputy führer will sit with the Jewish military lawyer from America. You are here to expedite my release to the Swiss." He then continued in perfect, if slightly accented, English. "Do you have word of my wife and son? Have they been informed of my safety?"

"I actually have no information to give you, Herr Hess. I am here to determine the validity of your statements." Gold then turned to the escorts and asked to be left alone with Hess.

"You understand the rules, Colonel. No physical contact and the prisoner is to remain seated."

"Yes, of course, now if you will excuse us."

Gold watched them leave and turned back to Hess.

"We are still being watched," Hess said.

"Yes, I understand that. If we could proceed?"

Hess dropped his voice to a whisper and said, "I have no intention of answering your questions. Since your government has been foolish enough to send you as their representative they are clearly not viewing my mission with the respect it warrants. I will however provide you with enough information to cause your president to give up his senseless support of the foolish Mr. Churchill."

Gold strained to hear what was being said and cupped his good ear.

"When I landed near Glasgow I was taken in by a plowman and his lovely mother; their name is McLean. While we sat in their cottage and waited for the military authorities to arrive I hid a photograph of my son on the underside of my chair. If you retrieve the photograph and split the paper you will find information that I am sure your scientists will be able to explain to your president. This is information I have kept from the British and their mad dog leader. And please, Colonel, if I may have the photograph returned to me by someone else. I do not intend to see you again."

Hess then knocked heavily on the table and called out for his keepers. The meeting was clearly over.

After Gold left and rode the elevator with all its machinations to the third floor he was met again by his now familiar escort.

"Your associates are in the warden's office. Would you like to bring a cup of tea? We can stop at the canteen on the way up."

"Thank you, no. Who is in the warden's office?"

"I'm afraid I can't say, sir, but they are expecting you."

As they climbed more stone stairs Gold wondered who could be expecting him. The permission to see Hess, signed by the prime minister himself, had been waiting for him at the embassy, and he had not mentioned or shown it to anyone. The only person who knew his destination and schedule was Miss Mary Wainwright of His Majesty's Service. For the first time, Gold wondered just which service that might be. When they reached the warden's office his escort, stepping aside, gestured for him to enter on his own. The room was filled with smoke and a voice known to all of England and much of the world was unmistakable.

"At last your forsaken colonel has arrived. Bar the door behind you and come join us." Sitting across a desk from the prime minister was Willie Sherman.

"Mr. Prime Minister, may I present Colonel Davidson of the Judge Advocate General's office."

"Sit, Colonel, we have been discussing our guest. I presume you had an informative visit with him. Of course even those with secret clearance believe he is being held at Mytchett Place, but that prisoner is a double, an impersonator. Actually a Jewish refugee from Hamburg. You have just met with the true representative of evil."

The meeting with Churchill and Sherman, although cordial, was unsatisfactory to all present. Sherman, who was representing the president, was in no position to exert any pressure on the prime minister, who was, of course, representing himself. Churchill believed little of what Hess had brought with him. He thought it all Hitler's diabolical attempt to intimidate him personally, to push him from office. That, if this atomic information or propaganda reached beyond the War Office, his support in commons would falter and a new prime minister might well sue for peace. Most British subjects had been convinced of the inevitability of this war and of the likelihood of victory. If they believed that Germany would soon have a single weapon making mass destruction and defeat unavoidable they would lose their resolve.

Sherman wanted to bring Hess to the United States where he could be questioned by the scientists working on the American bomb. Churchill refused, explaining that Hess was his trump card with Hitler, that the Germans knew he was in London and must fear what he might reveal of other matters, and that Hitler would have no way of knowing that Hess had not yet been broken and admitted that his trip was a hoax. When Sherman danced around the obvious question, Gold asked it directly.

"What if Hess is being truthful? What contingency plan do you suggest, Prime Minister?"

"There is no need for one," Churchill said, his face reddening with anger. "You Americans refuse to grasp the German character, Colonel. I have been forewarning the world of this man Hitler's satanic deeds for the past decade. Herr Hess is lying. He will never leave this island."

Sherman cringed at the prime minister's rage but Gold was unaffected. Although he had heard many accounts of the seemingly self-assured becoming flustered in the presence of great power, this was not a reaction Gold had ever experienced. In his adult years he had met many men of greatness and his reaction had always been the same. Interest in hearing their viewpoints and expressing his own. Never a sense of awe. He had often wondered about this lack of reaction. Was it that he did not respect their accomplishments or the motivation behind those accomplishments? Or was it based on his non-belonging, on his being Jewish in a Christian world? Morris had finally determined that it was something else, something not very complicated.

When he was a boy, living with his parents, he would occasionally carry his father's bag to appointments. The elder Goldstein's customers included many of the wealthiest inhabitants of Greenwich Village. Although they always used the servants' entrance, fittings were done in the private dressing rooms of these industrialists, bankers, and politicians. On these occasions Mr. Goldstein was in charge, he was not flustered and simply had a job to do. Often these great men would become uncomfortable and try to make conversation or small jokes but Morris's father, although polite, never faulted from his task.

"Do you dress right or dress left, sir?" It was the same with every customer, rich or poor. From velvet smoking jacket on Fifth Avenue to the wedding suit on Morton Street.

Morris came to understand that his father woke every morning to his own world, not the world of others, and that no one could make that world less important for him.

When Gold left the prison building he could see that although his car was still parked half on and half off the pavement, a bullish man in uniform was now holding the door for him.

"Good afternoon, sir, will it be back to the hotel then?" he said, touching the bill of his cap.

"No. Just drive around for a while. I want to see London."

"It's not such a pretty sight these days," the driver said, bouncing the car off the curb. "I have the *War Illustrated* here if you would like a look, but I suppose it's no more cheerful than looking out the windscreen. I read here that a deserter mailed his uniform back to his regiment postage due. Anything to help the war effort. If I deserted my missus would mail my uniform back with me in it."

A myriad of stories from this strange little newspaper followed by brief comments by this not very little driver. "Apparently the beer shortage may lead to a refusal of harvesters to work overtime."

"Understandable."

"I also read that we are buying 150 million tins of sardines from Portugal. A sly way for the government to import tin. And the salary paid some BBC announcers was over a thousand pounds a year."

Gold could not understand the expletive following that piece of war news.

"Do we have our destination yet, or do we continue to waste petrol? Not that it bothers me. I had my fill of it in Greece. Just happy to be alive and able to drive the gentleman around. Visiting a relative at Wormwood Scrubs Prison, were you, sir?"

With that, Gold could not resist.

"A prison? I thought it was one of your gentleman's clubs. Sergeant, you have lifted my spirits. Now tell me what became of my other driver, Miss Wainwright."

"Well, sir, I can't tell you the truth so I am left with lying or saying nothing. Which would you prefer?"

"Is she alright, I mean, did anything happen to her?"

"I really can't say, sir."

"Very well. Take me to the hotel."

After a seemingly roundabout trip through the

ruins of London they arrived at the Connaught. It was only then that Gold noticed his driver's face. A large purple burn scar covered the right side from his forehead to under his shirt collar, and his right eye was clearly glass. Gold instantly understood that the injury couldn't be much more than six months old, from when the Germans invaded Greece. What unimaginable horrors must this cheerful man have endured, how this dreadful injury must have changed his life. Could his "missus" still look adoringly at this once handsome face; could she keep the horror from her eyes? Did she love him that much? Had Gold himself done the right thing by not acknowledging, by hiding, *his* horror? Clearly this man knew the shock experienced by all who saw him. What was the right thing to do?

Walking into the hotel Gold thought of having a drink in the bar, felt a slight rush of anxiety at the possibility of Mary Wainwright being there waiting for him and turned away, not willing to allow his emotions or illusion to surface. Still trying to suppress thoughts of Mary, he walked to the front desk for his room key. There were three messages. The first was a wire, which read: ALL A'S STOP LOVE DAVID. The second, also a wire, read: CORRECTION STOP ONE A MINUS STOP LOVE DAVID. Both were from his son, David, whom he had told to send a wire whenever he had any important news to report. Gold could not help but wonder at a twelve-year-old's concept of important news in the middle of a war. The third message, on hotel stationery, was unsigned and read simply: "I think you are marvelous." When he asked who had delivered it he was told that the young woman, who had delivered all three from the embassy, had waited for him for quite some time and had just left. Gold's heart sank. While he was riding around bombed out London, Mary had been waiting for him, waiting to see him, to tell him that she had fallen for him. It was impossible of course, they had only known each other for a day. But he understood. He too felt taken. Unlike his love for his late wife, this was an instant connection, something he had never experienced before, something different from the close friendship and loving partnership he had developed with Ruth. This was what he had never before understood. A feeling without foundation, more than infatuation. No, not more, but so totally different.

The great Morris Gold, articulate, cultured, renowned for his almost lyrical legal briefs, was without definition. Stymied by the language he administered with such conceit. As though deserted by a dependable friend, Morris felt lost by the realization that his mastery of the language was imperfect; that he could not express what he was feeling. Love was something he believed in. The bond with Ruth had been based on mutual trust and respect. They had common goals. Their marriage was a good one, no, a wonderful one. Entered with the expectation of making a life and family together and they had succeeded. Ruth was a woman with whom he could discuss anything. She was his advocate and partner as he was hers. She knew the worst and best of him and still loved him. He had cherished her and now the memory of her. When she died, he had been determined to continue his life in the spirit of their relationship, as if she were watching over him, as if she still knew him so well. Ruth stood alongside Morris's father as both shepherd and judge of his actions. Ruth was the only person with whom he could discuss these feelings for Mary. They would have stayed up late arguing about the imperfect language. Ruth would have relentlessly probed his innermost thoughts to find the definition for his feelings. They would have discussed every possibility of his actions. What Ruth had called the "Is and Ts." The ifs and thens of life. By the time Morris reached his room he was in tears. Taking a cable blank from the desk he penciled a reply to David. MAZEL TOV YOUR MOTHER WOULD BE PROUD. HOME SOON. DAD

CONNAUGHT HOTEL
LONDON
OCTOBER 15, 1941

The telephone jarred him, was it Mary?

"Morris, it's Willie. I'm in the lobby. Be right up."

Sherman's voice brought the world back to Gold.

"Willie, give me ten minutes."

"It's important."

"And I need ten minutes," Gold said, hanging up the phone with a little more force than necessary.

While still washing his face—it couldn't have been more than three or four minutes later—there was a loud knock on the door. On opening it Gold could not help but laugh. There was Wild Willie Sherman dressed to the nines. Bowler hat and all.

"What the hell is so funny? After your performance with Churchill, I had to spend two hours at Downing Street being dressed down in front of every sniveling bureaucrat in the empire."

"Well, even though you look like Joe Kennedy's butler, I'm glad you're here. I was about to call you at

43

the embassy. But first, do me a favor and put that hat on for a minute."

"Go to hell. Let me in this room before I accept Churchill's offer to have you thrown in that cell with Hess."

"Come in, Willie, sit down. There's a new wrinkle I couldn't discuss in front of Churchill."

While Morris was still talking Sherman put his finger to his lips, indicating silence. He walked to the closet, put his bowler on the shelf, and removed a hanger. He meticulously hung his jacket, checking the lapels and pockets and stood brushing off some invisible lint and gesturing for Morris to follow him into the bathroom. Turning on the tub faucets he said, "Now you can talk, but keep your voice down. MI5 may be listening from the next room."

"Hess has offered us some information that he held back from the Brits," Gold continued, telling Sherman about his meeting with Hess, and the boy's hidden photograph in Scotland.

"He wants our attention, not the Brits'. Whatever his motivation, manipulation or sincerity, or a little of both, we are his target. I think the purpose of this entire escapade is to keep us out of the war. Whether his trip is with or without Hitler's endorsement is irrelevant. Equally irrelevant is whether the Germans have determined, as we have, that they will eventually lose the war if we become full participants."

Before acknowledging, Sherman stepped to the toilet, brushing his hand over his fly and looking down as if to check the fall of his trousers. He sat down weightlessly, as if sitting on a cushion.

"Morris, try to think like a German. Maybe they're simply trying to obtain a strategic advantage by creating conflict and mistrust between the United States and Britain."

"I have considered that. But I do not believe it to be the case. Hess is too important a player to waste on a ploy."

"In any case," Sherman said, "we are not at risk of losing our sovereignty as the British are."

"What's your point?"

"My point is that we really don't have that much to lose. Germany will never occupy the United States. It's a logistical impossibility. When the dust settles and this war is over, we will have to coexist with either one Europe under German rule or a fragmented Europe in ruins. Except for the loss of life, liberty and the pursuit of happiness in Europe, I'm not sure which is better for us."

"Ah, the crux of the situation rears its ugly political head. Would it be better for us to have Germany not as an enemy but as a strong economic competitor or even an economic partner, or to have a free Europe? All this brings us to the same conclusion. If Germany develops this bomb and we don't, we will forever be subject to their power. The United States would become a second rate power. And as we both know, second rate is no power at all. To coexist with Germany we must either destroy them, or not allow them to hold the bomb over us. We must determine the true status of the German bomb."

"I believe a little trip to Scotland is in order."

Gold started for the bedroom. "I'm going to get my car brought around and try to get an RAF flight."

Sherman jumped up to stop him. "No car, no driver, and no flight. All those drivers report everything we say and do back to MI5. We have to do this on our own. I have people here who can work out the details. When Frank Butler was here they assigned a beautiful woman as his driver. Do they really think we are so naïve? Morris, you look ill, don't tell me the Brits got to you with some bimbo."

"No. I'm just tired. My driver is a disfigured middle-aged sergeant."

"Well, don't trust him."

"OK, Willie, make the arrangement and let's get out of this place."

About an hour later Gold and Sherman were picked up outside the Connaught by a regular London taxi and driven to a printing house on Farrington Street. There, after walking through the press room and out a side door, they switched to an Alvis sedan and were taken via back streets to Paddington Station, where they ran to catch a train heading north. The only words spoken by the Alvis' driver after handing them tickets were, "Third stop." No reply was made as Sherman had indicated earlier that they should not speak until they were alone. Which they finally were on the platform at the third stop of the local.

Sherman spoke first. "A plane is waiting for us and we should be in Glasgow by midnight, where a car will take us to the McLean cottage. Do you know where the picture is?"

"I know that Hess said it's under the seat of one of the kitchen chairs. Beyond that we will see. This whole thing could be a ruse."

"I think not, Morris my boy. I only hope the McLeans will be as hospitable to us as they were to Hess. Did you read that account? The old lady said she had sat him by a warm fire and felt a need to mother him. Mother him? A warm fire? What is wrong with these people? Their cities are being bombed, their sons are being led to slaughter by inept, arrogant leaders, and they want to mother Hitler's deputy. My lord, what is it all about?"

"Willie, I have a friend, a criminal lawyer who defends the worst of us. I mean of we Americans. He works for the Legal Aid Society in New York. Well, Ted really becomes attached to his clients. Even those he knows to be guilty of the most heinous crimes. When Sallie the Knife was sentenced to death he wept. Sallie had tortured, raped, and killed a mother and daughter in front of the mother's eight-year-old little boy. Ted knew he was guilty of that and other atrocities, but he wept. That must be our car."

When the two men were finally bouncing down a narrow country lane it was almost sunrise. Although it had indeed been their car, the trip quickly became one fiasco after another. The driver couldn't find the airfield and by the time he did the rains had caused such deep ruts that the plane could not take off. Their Princetonian pilot hired a pair of gravediggers to smooth the field. The men stood ankle deep in the mud trying to find words that rhymed with Yorick and wondering who would bear whom on whose back just this once. While this was going on Sherman and Gold sat silently in an old wooden shed with a leaking tin roof. Unwilling to send the field overseer out in the rain, they were unable to speak of the one subject that occupied both their minds. Finally, after a harrowing flight they reached Glasgow, and surprisingly, found their driver waiting for them.

"It's the next turn off, just after Sheila's Nose."

"Whoever Sheila was, and why this piece of road was named for her nose, at least this driver seemed to know where he was going," thought Gold.

"Let me go first. I wouldn't want you fellows to get a face full of birdshot. Everyone is a bit nervous after our little invasion."

Gold and Sherman followed their driver to the door.

As he knocked he called out, "David, Mrs. McLean, it's Albert Bailey from the garage. I have some Yanks here wanting to meet you."

The door was opened by a frail elderly woman wearing a striped dressing gown.

"My lord, Albert. The three of you are soaked through and through. David, come at once and stoke the fire. Come in and get yourselves warm. David, where are you? Albert from the garage has brought us visitors. Americans. Now come sit by the fire."

"It's so kind of you to see us," Sherman said, obviously swept away by Mrs. McLean's mothering. "If our visit was not of the utmost importance we would never have intruded on you like this."

"Actually, I'm quite thrilled. We have become quite the international cottage. Envy of the whole village. Our first German visitor and now our first Americans. David! At last." David McLean, a tall, rather thin man in his early forties, had come in carrying a large bucket of coal.

"I am Mr. Sheridan and this is Mr. Levy," Sherman said. "We are with the International Red Cross and are charged with checking on the treatment of prisoners of war. Can you tell us how Herr Hess was treated when the authorities arrived?"

"I will tell you all about it, but first a cup of tea with a touch of something to warm us all up. Come sit here," she said, pointing to the four kitchen chairs.

Gold sat first, slipping his hands under the edges of the seat as he sat. He slightly shook his head to show Sherman that he had not found the picture. As Sherman sat his legs slipped out from under him and he ended up sprawled on the floor with a perfect view of the bottom of all four chairs.

David McLean jumped to the rescue, helping Sherman to his feet. "Maybe you've already tried a touch of our malt whiskey," he said with a grin.

"No, just a bad knee from the last war," Sherman answered. His expression told Gold that he had seen nothing under any of the chairs.

After Mrs. McLean had assured herself that her guests were properly dried out and comfortable she sent Albert off to get Mrs. Styles, her neighbor whose son had been captured in France and was a prisoner of war in Germany. While they waited, as Mrs. McLean did not want her friend to miss anything, Sherman, hoping to get a look around the house, asked if he could use the toilet. After being fitted with David's oilskins he was directed to the small shed about fifty feet of pouring rain from the kitchen door. Gold smiled to himself with the knowledge that Sherman was surely not going to find the picture under his next seat. Hess' instructions had been very specific. The picture, which Gold now believed did not exist, was supposed to have been under one of the kitchen chairs, not in the outhouse. Clearly a wasted trip, and now while Sherman was absent he had to make conversation with the McLeans. Morris asked about their farm and had a lengthy discussion with Mrs. McLean about each of the items on her mantel. Seven china commemorative plates, a picture of the late Mr. McLean in uniform from the last war, and a postal card of the king purchased on her one trip to Edinburgh. The wait seemed interminable. What was taking Sherman so long?

Sherman finally returned, but at the same moment as Albert arrived with Mrs. Styles. The kitchen was filled with steaming wet coats and there was a moment of confusion when Mrs. McLean went to the door and Morris offered his chair to Mrs. Styles even though both Sherman's and Albert's chairs were empty.

David, who had been standing silently in the corner eyeing Gold carefully, squeezed around everyone and left the kitchen only to return in a few moments carrying a fifth chair. When he lifted the chair over their heads to get back to his corner, both Sherman and Gold saw the little boy dressed in lederhosen.

"Let me give you a hand," Gold said, without a moment's thought. He took the chair from David McLean in one hand while peeling the picture off the bottom with the other. Before anyone, except an amazed Sherman, realized what had happened the picture was safely deposited in his jacket pocket and the chair was in the corner waiting for David McLean.

David smiled timidly and lowered himself into the chair. Once everyone was settled, except for Albert, who stood by the door, Mrs. McLean began to recount every detail of Hess' visit with frequent corrections by Mrs. Styles, who obviously had heard the story many times before and insisted on it being retold word for word. This was followed by a lengthy discussion of the treatment of POWs in Germany. Mrs. Styles questioned Sherman and Gold, the experts, on whether her son was receiving the mail and aid packages she had been sending through the International Red Cross. They assured her that prisoners were being well treated and that they were sure that her son appreciated everything she was doing for him.

An hour later, as they were leaving, David drew them aside and said, "I knew someone would come for that. I thought it would be a German spy but Albert's mother is American and we all know how he feels about you chaps. That's how I knew you two were authentic. High time you Yanks joined the war."

Almost immediately after leaving the McLean home Sherman was sitting doubled over and shirtless in the back of Albert's car.

"You're sure you want this little Nazi covering your rear?" Morris asked as he carefully, using Albert's first aid adhesive, adhered the photograph of the Hess child to Sherman's back. "And don't you think this is a little extreme. We haven't even looked for the microfilm. As far as we know it's just a picture of a little boy."

"I'm not interested in some Brit official with or without orders finding this."

"You're attached to the embassy. They can't search you."

"We could be searched and apologized to after it's too late. When we're safely aboard the plane we'll find out what we have here. Albert, is this as fast as we can go?"

"I can go faster if you want, but I didn't want to attract attention. 'Did you see Albert speed by with those two Yanks?' Before you know it the Yard or MI5 will be out here asking me questions. You two will be safe in Washington and—"

"You know best, Albert," Sherman interrupted. "Just do what you can."

NEW YORK CITY
OCTOBER 17, 1941

They were flown to the same field that Morris had landed at just a few days earlier. When he realized this his thoughts went to Mary and he experienced for the second time in his life that rush of emotion he had had first when reading her note. Their waiting plane took off almost immediately, giving him the chance to hold onto this feeling. Morris closed his eyes and let the roar of the engines and the vibrations of the fuselage block out the world. He sat back picturing their time together and re-creating in his mind their conversations. He let his feelings roll through him undefined and without clarification. His mind, no longer a censor of his emotions, became a cipher.

When the pilot came back to tell them they were over international waters, Morris returned to the world of others.

"Let's see what we have," Sherman said, taking off his shirt. "Morris, will you do the honors?"

Morris carefully began peeling the tape from Sherman's back.

"Oh for god's sake, I'm not a woman. Just rip it off."

Morris did as instructed, taking a quantity of hair and some skin with it. Wild Willie Sherman barely flinched.

With great care Sherman separated the Hess child's photograph from its postal card backing, exposing two small strips of film. When held up to the light they could only determine that one strip had three small frames and the other had four. Each frame was about half the size of a postage stamp. Sherman explained how these "microfilms," as he called them, had been seen before. The Germans had hidden them under the postage stamps on letters sent to their agents in the United States. Each frame could contain the contents of a whole page and could only be read through a microscope. Sherman took the larger filmstrip and carefully slipped it into the lining of his necktie, making sure it slid to the bottom of the short end and that it couldn't fall out.

"The silk stitching is very close together. Let me see yours," he said, lifting Morris's tie.

Using a small pocket knife Sherman cut open about half an inch of stitching on the back of Morris's tie. He slid the other filmstrip in and worked it down to the bottom with his fingers.

"A precaution," he said. "In the unlikely event that this contraption lands safely we should separate and meet at my office on Saturday."

"That will be fine," Morris answered. He then

sat silently thinking about his David and how disappointed he would be not to have their Saturday lunch. Should he not tell anyone he was home? He could go directly to Washington and then go home a few days later. David and his grandmother would never know and David would not be disappointed. Was it really that he didn't want to disappoint David? Was he thinking of doing this to spare David's feelings or to save himself from being the cause of David's disappointment? Or more accurately to save himself from David knowing that his father had made a choice. A choice that his son was to take second place. That's what he didn't want David to know.

Certainly Sherman could find an alternative way to get the film to Washington. It wasn't really necessary for him to be the delivery boy. But if he told Sherman he was not going to deliver the film he was sure that Sherman would try to make an issue of national security and patriotism. He would imply, or at least think, that Morris, being the son of immigrants, was less than devoted to America. No, it was being the son of Jewish immigrants, no not even that. It was being a Jew. Sherman would assume that he could not depend on or trust this Jew from New York. Morris made the decision not to say anything to Sherman. He would take the train directly to Washington and stay at the Willard, where he was unlikely to run into anyone he knew.

The flights took them to Iceland, then Greenland,

then Maine and finally New York, where Sherman was to change planes and continue on to Washington. A staff car driven by Major Blackstone met them at the plane and drove them into a hangar building just off the field. When the car had stopped Sherman tapped Blackstone on the shoulder and said, "I have an idea. Bob, switch ties with Morris here so he can go home and see his kid. You take the train from Penn Station and Morris, why don't you come down on Monday? It will take that long to figure out what we have on the microfilm."

Morris spent the weekend with his son. On Saturday they went to the newsreels and had lunch at Barney Greengrass as usual. Sunday morning Morris explained that he was going to Washington and that, over the objections of David's grandmother, David could stay in the apartment upstairs with Teresa, their housekeeper and cook.

David's mother had died after being struck by a New York City taxicab. She had turned David's pram around, in order to ease it down a particularly steep curb, and had stepped backwards into the path of the cab. A local pediatrician, walking up Broadway, tried to help but her injuries were too catastrophic and she died on the northeast corner of Eighty-sixth Street and Broadway. As she was hit she had let go of the pram. It was David's grandmother's belief that saving her child from certain death was her daughter's last selfless act. Although it had clearly not been his fault, the cab driver, a father of five, was inconsolable.

The Broadway community mourned with Morris and his family, and even today, twelve years later, people passed Morris and David with looks of sadness.

David had no memory of his mother and only knew her through the words of his father and his grandmother. According to them she was a most loving and loved woman, she adored her one child and was looking forward to teaching him the many skills that she excelled in. From horseback riding and rowing, to drawing and reciting Shakespeare, she had clearly been a woman of great achievement. David sometimes thought that maybe it would have been better if she had been a mean and stupid person. Then he would not feel like he was missing so much and his Dad wouldn't be so sad about her dying. He had once told this to Teresa, who had warned him never to tell this thought to his father or to his grandmother. It would make them very angry.

David wanted his father to come home soon. Although he loved his grandmother, Ruth's mother, she was even more protective of him than his Dad was. He hadn't been allowed to go out alone after dark and worst of all he wasn't allowed to go to the movies on Eighty-third Street. This had been their tradition. Every Saturday morning David and Morris would go to the newsreels and then, during their walk up to Barney Greengrass, where they would have lunch, discuss what they had seen. It was always herring in sour cream with black bread for Morris and lox and cream cheese on the same black bread for David. David knew, although he hadn't told his father, that he would never get close to, let alone taste, herring. He managed to survive lunch by keeping his eyes fixed on his father's forehead. This way, if he really concentrated, he wouldn't have to see the slimy white and gray mass going into his father's mouth. This trick also led Morris to believe that he had David's undivided attention, a bonus that did not escape David's notice.

David also wanted to be back in his own room, in their own apartment, two flights up from his grandmother, where he could peer at slides through his microscope and get an occasional sneak look at Teresa getting dressed in the morning.

The day before Morris left for England, he and David had spent their usual Saturday morning together. During their walk uptown after watching the newsreels, Morris tried to explain his new job to David.

"David, I have taken on a client who requires me to travel extensively."

"Is it the government, Dad. Are we going to go to the White House again?" David had asked.

"Did you enjoy that trip, when you met the president and Mrs. Roosevelt?"

"It was a long time ago and I was just a kid. So I guess what I liked most was playing with their dog, Fala, and that man who took care of him."

"You mean Tom Quinn. You liked him, didn't you?"

Watching the three of them at the time, Morris had wondered if Quinn was protecting Fala, watching David, or just having a good time playing with both of them.

Quinn was a true "old-timer," having been assigned to the presidential detail in '32. It was said that Quinn and the president had silent signals, which they exchanged. Some were sure these signals were used during Friday night poker games. The president was unnaturally lucky at cards.

"I did like him. He told me all about the counterfeiters he had caught before he worked for the president. One of the smartest was named Gold, just like us. And he said if I studied hard I could grow up to be a smart Jew lawyer just like you, Dad."

Morris stopped walking and gently holding his son's shoulders asked, "What do you think he meant by that?"

"I don't know. Mr. Quinn is pretty smart too. Maybe I want to be a Secret Service man like him."

Letting go of David's shoulders Morris said, "I think we should continue this conversation over lunch when I have your undivided attention."

At lunch Morris had talked about thousands of years of prejudice against the Jews, from the Egyptian pharaohs and the Spanish inquisition to the present and Germany under Hitler. He discussed how the Jews were blamed for the crucifixion and how they were accused of killing Christian babies during Passover. This kind of prejudice, he told his son, although wrong in any place or time, was totally unacceptable in America. Morris then had explained how the Supreme Court enforced the constitution, how the constitution protected all Americans, and how some of the great justices had been Jews.

After lunch David still couldn't grasp the difference between Mr. Quinn calling his father a smart Jew lawyer and his father calling Mr. Quinn a good Irish cop.

On the walk home both David and Morris, although not talking, were thinking about the same thing. A year earlier they had not gone to the newsreels one Saturday morning because David was waiting to hear about his inevitable selection as shortstop for the school team. The coach had promised to call all new team members by 10 A.M. so they could meet in Central Park and pass out the uniforms. The school colors were black and orange, just like the Giants.

His father had actually taken the time to help him practice. They went to Riverside Park as that was the place none of his schoolmates would be likely to see them. Morris actually took off his jacket and laid it on a park bench. For David it did not matter that his father could not hit grounders to him, or that he really couldn't catch the ball when David threw it back. All that mattered was that his friends not see his father in his shirt and tie throwing grounders to him because he couldn't hit the ball, or David running the ball back to his father because he couldn't catch.

When no call came by lunchtime David knew that in spite of being one of the best hitters and fielders he had not made the team. Lunch at home was a somber affair. After a long silence Morris had said, "David, my son, I am so very sorry that this has happened. If only I had been able to spend more time throwing you those grounders, if only we had more time together or your mother was still alive. I'm sure she would have been able to hit the perfect grounders. I am so very sorry, David."

"It's not that. Grandma understands. She says it's because there are no Jewish kids on the team. She wants you to talk to the coach but please Dad, don't. Actually she said you should call the president and tell him. Wouldn't that be something?"

"David, I can't..."

"Come on, Dad, I know that. I just think it would be funny to have the president call the coach and ask why his best player didn't make the team."

Morris, reaching across the table for David's hand, had said, "I don't want you to think that being Jewish will hold you back. This is a great country and you can achieve anything you are capable of achieving."

With tears running down his face David pushed his father's hand away and sobbed, "That's not true, it's a stupid lie. I'm capable of being on the team and I'm not on it."

With that David ran from the table and slammed the

door to his room with such force that it would require repainting. Morris was left trying to figure out why he had made such a meaningless statement to his son. In fact, David was right. It was a lie. Although America was remarkable in many ways, it certainly was not a utopia of equality. It would be several months after David had changed schools before he received a large envelope from the White House with an inscribed photograph of the president.

"To David, the best shortstop on my team. Your friend, FDR."

WASHINGTON, D.C.
OCTOBER 20, 1941

On Monday when Morris was escorted into Sherman's office he could tell that the news was not good.

"Morris, you had better sit," Sherman said, pointing to the wingback chair while he did his now familiar dance around the office. "The Hess documents were brilliantly constructed. They prove that the Germans are far ahead of us while apparently giving us nothing that our scientists can use. We meet with the president at nine tonight but first we have a decision to make. What is our most critical task? Stopping the Germans or making our own super-bomb?"

"Bill, I don't think—" Morris started to answer.

"Wait, don't answer yet, I have put a lot of thought into this and want to present my case first. If we develop this bomb and are unsuccessful in stopping the Germans, we have a stalemate of sorts. A barely acceptable situation. Two great powers each in constant fear of a devastating sneak attack from the other and at the same time afraid of attacking each other for fear of incredible retaliation. Hitler would get control of Europe and we could control the Americas and probably, if we show Japan what we have, control the Far East. Africa would be up for grabs. Russia, being so vast, may be able to hold on and stay out of it, but I just don't see Adolf leaving Uncle Joe alone.

"I don't think I have to describe the consequences of our failure to stop the Germans before we develop our own super-bomb. It seems to me that our best option is to put our greatest efforts into stopping Germany. If we succeed in stopping them it makes the question of our success in developing the bomb moot. If no one else has it, we don't need it."

Sherman was actually disappointed when all Gold said was, "Willie, I couldn't agree with you more."

That afternoon the two of them met with the president and General Marshall. Much to Sherman's surprise everyone had reached the same conclusions as his own. It was agreed that the preliminary task of planning the development of this new weapon would be assigned to the Army. The general would conduct a private search for the military officer most suited to plan and direct the project. The president explained that although this officer would need to have some scientific background, of the utmost importance would be his ability to enlist, lead, and command the most brilliant minds in the country. He would also have to be able to accept that he would be out of the chain of command. His work would be of such a secret nature that promotion would not be possible until the project was finished. And then only if he were successful. The best he could expect from failure would be the end of his military career.

It was also agreed that Sherman's office would be

responsible for the clandestine activities of stopping the German bomb, with the armed forces giving all assistance as requested. The president added two caveats. First, in order to prevent disagreement or unnecessary delays, the president made it clear that Morris Gold was the final authority and had the power to act in his name. Second, that all notes and records of this meeting were to be destroyed. This meeting had never happened and FDR added as a joke, "The president and General Marshall did not attend the meeting that never was."

Morris knew that this was not the time to remind the president that without the written executive order he had been promised he was still a private citizen and could be held criminally responsible for many of his actions. He also fully understood that political and diplomatic pressures might make it expedient for FDR to deny his authorization. Being arrested in England as a spy during wartime, let alone being charged in the United States with embezzlement of government funds, did not appeal to him. He would certainly have to receive the executive order before he expensed any government monies or left the country again.

Morris returned to the White House that evening for an early dinner. In the family dining room with its oval claw-foot table and the painting of George Washington seemingly looking at himself in the mirror across the room, the president, Eleanor and their son, James, one of FDR's closest advisors, were already seated. Morris had known Jimmy since Al Smith's 1928 campaign for the presidency. Together they told the story, repeatedly interrupting each other, of how, wearing Smith for President campaign buttons, they had narrowly escaped an anti-Catholic mob that chased them from Lüchow's restaurant, across Fourteenth Street, up Second Avenue, and west on Seventeenth. When they stopped to catch their breath, Jimmy turned to Morris, with that smile so reminiscent of his father's, and said, "That's what I get for associating with my parents' friends." Every time they recounted the story the mob got larger and the run longer. It was repeated to great laughter whenever they were together with Jimmy's parents.

Dinner was fish chowder and grilled cheese sandwiches, the president's favorites. After all the questions of family and friends had been exhausted, the president removed two folded documents from his jacket pocket. The first, which he passed on to Morris, was a handwritten presidential pardon for "all violations of law committed by Morris Gold in the service of his country."

"Mo, I'm afraid this is the best I can do for you. And even this inadequate document must be kept secret from everyone, including Willie Sherman. Eleanor and Jimmy have already read it. They will be your witnesses of its existence." The president then reached over and took it back from Morris, touched its corner with his lighter, and dropped the flaming paper on his plate. He then took the other document and without unfolding it added it to the flames.

Morris realized he should never underestimate his good friend's shrewdness or ability to dissatisfy all parties in an acceptable way. It was actually brilliant. The president had the two people he trusted most protecting his interest, and for Morris, these same two people, whose integrity and intelligence he trusted immensely, would be there to protect him should something go wrong. He had no choice but to accept this less than perfect arrangement. After dinner Eleanor excused herself, and Morris, Jimmy, and the president retired to the family living room. The argument that ensued between Jimmy and his father was soon settled when FDR agreed to making the martinis Jimmy's way: three parts gin and one part vermouth but with two drops of absinthe and both olives and lemon peel, as the president preferred. Another Roosevelt compromise with no one completely satisfied. FDR clearly deserved his reputation for making the worst tasting martinis anyone had ever had.

The evening's discussion began with Morris describing in more detail his meetings with Hess and Einstein and the contents of the microfilm. The president was most concerned about the implications of the British finding out the extent of Germany's progress on the super-bomb and what that would do to the war effort. Then he explained Jimmy's new job as liaison between the various intelligence arms of the government.

"The whole process of collecting intelligence must be reorganized," the president said. "Right now it all comes from an ad hoc league of opposing teams playing at the same time, on the same field, and all with the same goal line. As my good and articulate friend Morris Gold would say, 'It's a can of worms.' We are going to replace this muddle with something akin to the British MI5. But that will take the one thing we don't have. Time. Concentrate on what we must do now. It is imperative that our first priority must be keeping Winston in the dark. This is for you to do. I don't want the details of how you accomplish this, I just want to be briefed on the problems and results." With that he levered himself to a standing position, locked his leg braces, and said, "I'm going to leave you boys to it. Jimmy, would you ask Tom Quinn to take me downstairs? I have a poker game that can't start without me."

Morris understood that James Roosevelt was not without his own political savvy. His appointment to coordinate the Army, the War Department, the FBI, and all the other intelligence gathering organizations was a good one. Without the friction of technically outranking the older and more experienced bureaucrats he would be trying to get cooperation from, he still held, if needed, the unspoken royal rank of being the president's son.

They both agreed with the president's view that their first priority was to prevent the spread of the Hess information.

"We don't have much time, we have to find a way to stop the British interrogation of Hess. They will inevitably break him down and he will reveal everything. Ten days or two weeks at the most. I have considered, and my father knows nothing of this, causing his death in prison, but the risk is too great. If MI5 ever found out that we were responsible it would cause a major rift with them and we are going to need their trust, and their assistance rebuilding our own intelligence network. It will have to be something more subtle."

"The word is murder, not 'causing his death.' Are we really that superior that we are able to consider murdering an incarcerated man? Hess is no longer active in the war. He is a prisoner of war. He can do no harm short of causing a problem that would soon be forgotten, or at least forgiven. I know it's a war but let's not become what we are fighting against."

"I'm not sure I'm ready to accept your analysis of wartime morality, but we do both agree on one thing—we need to stop the interrogations. There may be a solution available to us. There is a new drug, it's called sodium thiopental. Our FBI director told me about it. He was considering using it on German spies but J. Edgar probably prefers using it on his boys. It was first developed as a substitute for ether in dental surgery but it was also found to be a kind of truth drug, relieving patients of conscious control of their reticence to reveal the truth. The problem, and here is how it may work for us, is that if administered in too high a dose it causes damage to the brain. A loss of mental ability. The risk is that an overdose can also cause death, which would bring us back to a situation we both want to avoid."

"So if it works, it's a lesser death, maybe not preferable to the victim but maybe more acceptable to us. Does the recipient ever recover?"

Looking to his left, which was the tell that Morris knew from playing poker with him, Jimmy replied, "I think that's a possibility."

"Can you find out more about the actual mortality risk without involving Hoover?"

"I'll make an appointment with father's dentist and discuss the risks to the president should it be administered to him."

NEW YORK CITY
OCTOBER 23, 1941

They had chosen the Waldorf Astoria as their New York meeting place. Willie Sherman seemed to have an unlimited supply of money and knew everyone in the hotel. Their rooms in the tower always had fresh flowers, coffee, and a fully stocked bar. Once again, however, Willie would hold discussions only in the bathroom with the tub running full force. In New York, at the Waldorf, it was the FBI and not MI5 he was concerned about. When Morris first told him about the sodium thiopental his only comment was, "That's J. Edgar's boy drug, isn't it?"

"Am I the only one who doesn't know something about the director?" asked Morris. "I would think this would be in the category of top secret. Jimmy Roosevelt used almost the same words. I didn't really understand what he meant by it at the time, but now I do. I don't like the man and at our only meeting he made it quite clear that he was not fond of New Yorkers, but are we really saying he's a fairy?"

"No question. I've seen the pictures. But more importantly, he's evil. And it's not New Yorkers he doesn't like. It's something else about you he doesn't like. In fact, some of his best friends are New Yorkers, if you understand what I'm saying. Walter Winchell feeds him tips on fixed races, which he gets from the mob. Hoover then places bets with the same mob and wins most of the time. He's in bed with those guys. It's a treaty of sorts. Hoover has the dope on them and they have the photographs of him. If he didn't have so much dirt on everyone else he would have been exposed a long time ago."

"I don't believe that the president knows about this."

Reaching to turn off the tub, Sherman said, "And I can't believe he doesn't. Hoover must have something on the boss. It's almost time for our dentist appointment. We should leave now."

While Morris left the Waldorf first, using the Fiftieth Street entrance, Willie used the basement and eventually came out on Forty-ninth. Their dentist appointment was at Brooks Brothers on Madison Avenue and Forty-fourth Street. Both men wandered downtown slowly, trying to see if they were being followed. They then circled the block in opposite directions in order to meet each other at the entrance to Brooks on Madison Avenue. The theory being that anyone following them would have to be jammed up in the entrance to the store and not have a chance to follow them upstairs.

When they finally arrived at a private fitting room on the third floor they were met by a middle-aged and rumpled man who had blood spatter on his shirt collar. He was obviously not a Brooks Brothers customer.

Without giving them his name he set a black medical bag on the fitting room bench and proceeded to brief Gold and Sherman on the use of sodium thiopental, just how many vials would accomplish their goal and how to inject them without leaving any visible puncture marks. He then opened his bag and removed six vials of the drug and two hypodermic syringes. As he was leaving he turned to Gold and said, "Don't forget to keep everything sterile. We wouldn't want your patient to become infected."

That evening, back at the Waldorf, Morris and Willie developed several elaborate scenarios for administering the drug to Hess, but none had seemed plausible. The decision was made to go to London and make a plan once there.

That evening Morris went home and told David that he would be leaving on business for a week, and maybe longer, and that he should listen to his grandma and Teresa and not worry. David, not being fooled by any of it, clicked to attention and gave his father a crisp salute as he walked out the door.

LONDON
OCTOBER 24, 1941

Morris was still amazed at the progress of technology. Instead of a long sea voyage he could now fly from New York to England with only two stops. First in Montreal and then Gander, Newfoundland. Flying long distances was now not the province of adventures but a routine event for anyone connected with the government. You either hitched a ride with a ferry pilot delivering a new bomber or if you were lucky, or unlucky as some would say, in a plush VIP version of a troop transport with a congressman or industrialist on a fact-finding mission. Morris always tried to avoid the latter, as he trusted the discretion of a young woman pilot from Duluth or Peoria far more than some inflated VIP. He also preferred the company.

This trip, however, was different. Willie had arranged for him to have the plane almost to himself, a Boeing Flying Boat, and although it had a range of 3,500 miles and could have made the flight nonstop, they had refueled in Gander. The other passengers were a young couple in stylish clothes and a beefy man in his forties who sat with a .45 caliber pistol on his lap. The couple occasionally whispered to each other, but Morris could not hear them well enough to even determine what language they were speaking. The pilot was a young man from Albany, New York, whose first flying experience had been helping his father, a retired doctor, take aerial photographs of New England.

After a brief conversation about the splendors of autumn in New England, Morris was able to close his eyes and try to review the upcoming mission. There was not much to review as the plan only went as far as meeting Sherman in London. By the time they had reached Gander, Morris had reconsidered all his conversations with Willie, all the arguments and debates, and still had no idea what to do.

Then, watching the pilot leave the plane with his leather camera case around his neck, he had an idea that just might work. By the time they took off again Morris had worked out the details. It involved his son David's hidden ball trick. You had to make someone think the other guy had the ball while it was actually in your own leather mitt. For the rest of the trip Morris slept, and chatted with the pilot and copilot. He found himself to be in a cheerful mood. Maybe someday he would be able to tell David how his trick had helped save the world.

When they reached Foynes, in neutral Ireland, the Shannon estuary was fogged in. The pilot, accustomed to foggy landings on the coast of Maine, brought the Clipper in with hardly a bump and taxied to the dock. Although the plan was for Morris to fly from Foynes to Croydon airfield in London, there was Willie Sherman waiting behind the wheel of a black Cadillac sedan with an American flag flying from its fender. Not what Morris expected for a clandestine arrival. He threw his bag on the back seat and got in the front. Before he could get his door closed, Sherman accelerated onto the gravel roadway and said, "Sometimes it's better to not look like you're trying to hide anything."

"Willie, remember to keep to the left."

"I've been voting for the old man since thirty-two."

"And I would like to see my son again, so keep the car on the wrong side of the road."

"I've done this before. Drove a truck here in seventeen. Don't worry. This will give us time to work out getting the drugs into the bastard. The car is the safest place not to be overheard."

"Where are we going?"

"An unpronounceable airfield southwest of Dublin. Should take us about four hours, then a cramped flight, courtesy of the RAF, to London. Colonel Davidson and the president's special representative, as myself, have an appointment at Wormwood Scrubs Prison.

"There is something you should know before we discuss plans. Churchill, in order to protect British POWs, has now publicly ordered that Hess be strictly isolated and protected, but treated with the utmost of dignity.

"The British have accommodated this by having a double, a Jewish German émigré posing as Hess, held in isolation and, one would hope, being treated with the utmost dignity. First he, the double that is, was taken to the Tower of London, then he was moved under false security to Mayhill army barracks. I don't know his next move but I do know that our Rudolph Hess, the genuine article, is still where Churchill wants him. At Wormwood Scrubs Prison where all means of interrogation can and are being used."

"Do you think we will be in time?"

"Apparently Hess has revealed many choice pieces of information about Hitler and his mates, but nothing about the bomb. I think he is waiting for us to respond to the microfilm."

Morris then slipped the photograph of Rudolph and little Wolf Hess from his pocket. Hess was swinging his little blond boy by the arms and both were laughing.

Looking over, Sherman said, "Well, enjoy your little memory, Herr Hess. It just might be your last for quite some time."

After replacing the photograph in his jacket pocket Morris closed his eyes and said, "I have a plan."

"Well, don't hold back any longer."

With that Morris explained his strategy for how they could inject Hess and escape without becoming suspects. By the time they finished examining and refining Morris's idea they were approaching the outskirts of Dublin.

"There is one more issue on our agenda. A British liaison officer assigned to our embassy has been asking about you. Seems he wants to know when Colonel Davidson might be returning to London. He claims to have enjoyed your company during some military ball that you and I know you never attended. Maybe it's just a mistaken identity but it could be MI5 trying to find out more about you. Hopefully we can accomplish our mission quickly and quietly and get out town before they do."

"I have no idea what this is about. Do you recall his name?"

"General...? No, vice something. I've got it! Air Vice-Marshal Forrest something. Wainwright, that's it. Air Vice-Marshal Forrest-Wainwright. I always have trouble with the second half of these hyphenated names."

Morris closed his eyes and said nothing. He had been trying to keep thoughts of Mary Wainwright out of his consciousness but really had only succeeded in keeping her out of his wakefulness. Many nights during the past two weeks his sleep had been interrupted by her presence. Sometimes to his annoyance, but more often to his pleasure.

With his eyes still closed he said, "Why don't I meet with him and find out what they're up to. If it's all a mistake Wainwright will be mildly embarrassed and if not maybe we can learn something from him. Tell the embassy he can reach me at the Connaught. It might also give us some cover after we see Hess."

"So much for getting out of town," Willie laughed. "You're becoming quite the spy."

When they arrived at the airstrip Willie parked the

car, rolled up the flag, put it in his coat pocket, and put the ignition key on top of the left front tire. The plane, a small three-seater, was already warming up. They walked over, climbed into the two canvas seats behind the pilot, who, yelling over the engine noise said, "It's a de Havilland Leopard Moth, she's fast enough for what she is and should get us over London in about three hours, clear skies all the way. There's a Thermos vacuum flask with hot coffee between the seats. Thought you Yanks would like that. But I would wait until we level off at five thousand feet before you open it. And open it slowly. They tend to explode a little."

He then raced the engine, released the brakes, and was airborne within seconds. After a few minutes he reached back and tapped Gold on the knee and then pointed out the side window.

Looking down on the Irish Sea they could see what appeared to be merchant vessels accompanied by small warships. Gold guessed that these were some of the destroyers transferred to the British under the Lend-Lease Act, and that the merchant ships contained materiel from the States. The pilot then pointed up and yelled, "Spitfires checking up on us. Let me give them a wag so we don't get shot down." He then rocked the plane side to side and waved out his window. "They may follow us for a while but I don't think it will be a problem. Just in case though, do you lads know how to swim?"

One of the Spitfires did follow them until they were

well over land and then gave a wag of its own before flying off.

The weather was still clear for their landing outside of London. A couple of high bumps and they were on the ground rolling toward the hangar buildings. The pilot cut the engine and came to a stop just in front of a waiting Rolls Royce.

As they jumped down the pilot said, "There's a toilet and sink in the hangar behind us. It's been a pleasure flying you Yanks, I hope to see many more of you in short order. Welcome to England." He then trotted off toward a group of laughing pilots standing around a young woman in flight gear.

After they had both used the much-needed facilities Sherman took the American flag out of his pocket and attached it to the fender of the waiting car.

"Get in so we can be on American soil. This car is now part of the embassy." After Morris had settled into his seat Sherman tapped on the glass partition behind the driver. "Get us to the embassy."

On arrival they went directly to the basement and a small secure room that looked like a holding cell. Here they repeatedly practiced their scheme and at one point had one of the embassy's Marine detachment stand in as one of Hess' prison guards. Both knew that they had only five or six seconds to complete their task. Any longer and they were sure to be caught, with unthinkable consequences.

WORMWOOD SCRUBS PRISON
OCTOBER 25, 1941

Nothing had changed except for the weather, which was now colder and overcast with an occasional light rain. The side door still had the sign that had so amused Gold and the same warder who had been inside the entrance on his prior visit asked them to fill in the visitors' book and did a search of their clothing. Gold had hidden the serum-filled syringe in the lining of his officers' hat and Sherman had brought a distraction: a parcel of Hershey bars and cigarette packs, which he tried to convince the warder to let him give to Hess. After finally relinquishing the package they were escorted up the stairs to the lift.

It delivered them to a different floor than before. They entered a long hallway with six open cell doors on each side. At the end of the hall was a steel door with a small peephole. A guard was sitting on a wooden chair to the left of the door. As they approached he got up, slid the bolt, and held the door open for them to enter ahead of him. When Sherman and Gold entered the room Hess, standing in front of his chair, was clearly awaiting their arrival. He was wearing a gray prison uniform, was perhaps a little heavier and appeared less pale. His head had been shaved at some point as it now showed a stubble of no longer than a half inch.

The order to sit that came from the guard was instantly obeyed.

Gold took his hat from under his arm and handed it to Sherman. Turning to the guard standing behind him and taking the photograph from his pocket, he said, "I would like to give this to the prisoner. It's a photograph of him and his son in what I'm sure were happier times for both of them."

"Nothing may be passed to the prisoner."

With that Gold moved squarely in front of the guard and said, in his best imitation of an irate officer, "This is not possible, Sergeant, do you know who we are? We have also brought a package of chocolates and cigarettes from the Red Cross, which you people confiscated. Are you denying this man a picture of his son and some simple treats permitted under the conventions of war? Is this how you want your fellow troops to be treated by the Germans? I demand that you bring our package here immediately." By this time Gold's face was only inches away from the guard's and he had his view of Sherman and Hess completely blocked. It was a colonel dressing down an enlisted man. Every time the sergeant tried to answer Gold would move even closer and raise his voice more. He now had his undivided attention.

With Gold blocking the guard's view, Sherman, the syringe already in hand, reached across the table, grabbed Hess' right wrist, and thrust the needle between his thumb and first finger, plunging the serum into him as rapidly as he could. Within seconds the empty syringe was in Sherman's pocket. Hess hardly had a chance to react, so fast was Sherman's well practiced move. No more than a whimper came from him before he brought both hands to his face and moaned.

The guard, hearing this, was indecisive about pushing this American officer out of the way so he tried to move around him while he was still being dressed down by the American colonel. "Do not turn away from me, Sergeant. I am still—"

Sherman interrupted. "Let's settle down here. After all, we're on the same side, and it appears this little argument has been too much for our prisoner. He looks upset."

Hess looked confused, as if he did not know what to do. He stared at the three men facing him without saying a word.

Sherman, putting his hand on the sergeant's shoulder, said, "Why don't we forget this little incident. I'm sure Colonel Davidson has no desire to lodge a complaint. Best it all be forgotten. We will leave the photograph and the parcel with your commanding officer and explain how exemplary you have been in following your orders. We have only a few questions to ask the prisoner but you may stay in the cell if you wish."

Gold then removed a typed list of questions from his jacket pocket and began, in German, what appeared to be a basic interrogation.

"Are you Reich minister Rudolph Hess?"

"Were you born in Alexandria, Egypt?"

"Are you married to Ilsi Prohl Hess?"

With each question Hess merely nodded his head as if answering in the affirmative. When they reached questions requiring more complex thought Hess seemed confused.

"Did you fly to Scotland with a proposal for peace?"

No response.

"Are you representing the führer on this mission?"

"I wish to go outside, Papa is waiting for me."

Sherman nodded to Gold and both men stood to leave.

Hess said, "You should be careful walking with the dogs."

Turning to the guard, Sherman said, "I think he has had enough for today. We will report your excellent adherence to orders. Our misunderstanding is forgotten. Thank you again, Sergeant." With Gold and the sergeant exchanging crisp salutes the visit was over.

When they walked out of Wormwood Scrubs Prison, although the street was still wet, the sun was just breaking through the dark clouds. Sherman put his arm around Gold's shoulders. "Maybe there is reason for a sunny day. Let's get to the embassy in case this backfires on us. I didn't like the look of those empty cells. This isn't a place for us to spend very much time." He waved to their waiting car with its American flag, which backed down the narrow road and stopped in front of them. As they climbed in Gold tossed his officers' cap on the floor and said, "I hope I will never need this again."

"Don't be so morose. In like a charm, Hess drugged and still alive, and out without being caught. I'd call it a 'hat trick' all around."

"Not so fast, Willie, we're still under the lion. Tower of London, chopping block, and all that."

"This automobile represents sovereign territory of the United States of America, we are protected here and in the embassy. Then our flight home, maybe chased by Spitfires, but not shot down I'm sure."

Gold sat back in the plush seat of the embassy car, closed his eyes, and thought about the events of the past few months. He wanted to get home and spend time with his son but also had unfinished business in London. The message from Air Vice-Marshal Forrest-Wainwright was probably in relation to the war effort, but possibly a father's aid to his daughter, or a father protecting his daughter and telling Gold to stay away. After all, a middle-aged Jewish-American widower with a young son was not the man of a father's dreams. Tapping on the glass partition to get the drivers attention, he said, "Drop me off at the Connaught."

Having checked into his now familiar rooms Morris called the embassy to have his luggage brought back to the Connaught along with any messages waiting for his attention. He then bathed and wrapped himself in the voluminous Turkish towel and waited for his bags to arrive.

Somehow, along with his luggage stored at the embassy was his small bag from the flight over. Gold changed into his Army uniform and was once again Colonel Davidson of the Judge Advocate's office. The sealed pouch of messages from the embassy signals room contained several coded letters from Washington, which Morris examined after laboriously decoding them. He knew which were of high priority by the form of address and salutation. The others could wait. These double coded messages he then decoded again with a onetime formula known only to himself and Mr. Webster in the White House. It was a simple code but impossible to break without the key. He had only met Mr. Webster, or whatever his real name was, once, and even then they communicated through a closed door in the White House basement. He would never be able to identify Webster by real name or appearance. Thus protecting many other clients of the master code maker.

The first double encoded message was based on information given to the president by Maxim Litvinov, the Soviet ambassador to the United States. The information was directly from Stalin. Morris had known Litvinov for some time. His mother-in-law, Ruth's mother, was a close friend of Litvinov's British wife, Ivy Lowe, daughter of Walter Lowe, the Jewish writer. The families had attended celebrations together and Morris had sat with the elder statesman often discussing Jewish life in the United States, Britain, and the Soviet Union, but always laughing over the routines of Harpo Marx.

Marx had been sent to the Soviet Union as a good-will ambassador after Litvinov had helped convince FDR to recognize the Soviet Union in 1933. Sometimes the old diplomat would mime the routine he had performed with the American comedian who was now a friend. Being a Jew, Litvinov had been in and out of government and in and out of prison. But he was a true international insider, having been exiled to Switzerland, arrested in France, deported to England, and appointed the roaming ambassador for the Soviet government. More than any other Soviet diplomat, Litvinov was to be trusted.

The information in the first message was that the Soviets had infiltrated the German research facility in Leipzig that was directed by Werner Karl Heisenberg, a German theoretical physicist known by Einstein.

It claimed that the progress being made was substantial and that although they were getting information from one of the scientists he was unwilling to commit sabotage.

The attached analysis from the White House claimed that the Russians were disinclined to destroy the facility without first acquiring the research for themselves, not that their contact was unwilling to commit sabotage.

Morris knew that although Litvinov was to be trusted this information had merely been conveyed by him after extensive revisions by the Soviets. The problem was now not only the Germans getting the bomb but the possibility of the Russians getting it as well.

The other double encrypted communiqué was from the president himself. Apparently he had shared the Soviet information with Churchill and it was Churchill's interpretation that the Russians were being disingenuous and not to be trusted. Particularly that "clever little Hebrew, Litvinov." Gold's view of Litvinov was different.

The third message, not encrypted, was a reply to a note he had asked the embassy to deliver. His meeting with Air Vice-Marshal Forrest-Wainwright was, as he had requested, set for 9:00 A.M. The air vice-marshal's aide-de-camp had arranged to have him picked up at the hotel at 8:30 and then driven to the Savoy for a private meeting over breakfast.

The next morning as he came out of the lift he saw a decorated senior officer, in RAF uniform, standing by the entrance. He had not seen Mary since she had driven him to Wormwood Scrubs Prison so long ago, but there she was, in her unadorned uniform in the lobby of the Connaught, standing next to the officer who he assumed to be her father. She took Morris' breath away.

"Colonel Davidson, may I introduce Air Vice-Marshal George Forrest-Wainwright of the Royal Air Force."

The air vice-marshal, noting Morris' obvious confusion over whether to salute or shake hands, said with a wry smile, "No need for formality, Colonel, it just draws attention and the RAF has enough to do without pomp and ceremonial gestures. I believe you know my daughter."

The air vice-marshal, not as tall as Morris, had a full head of gray hair and a well healed crescent shaped scar above his left eye. Some of the ribbons on his chest clearly represented decorations from the great war, the most prominent being the Victoria Cross, the highest British award for bravery, equal to the American Congressional Medal of Honor.

Morris recognized the VC from his international law school course. It was a classic story of British lore, that although most awards could be rescinded for later criminal misdeeds, the Victoria Cross could never be withdrawn. King George V had felt so strongly that no matter the crime committed by anyone on whom the VC has been conferred, the decoration should not be forfeited. Even were a Victoria Cross recipient to be sentenced to death for murder, he should be allowed to wear the VC on the scaffold.

"Yes, of course, my most competent driver on several occasions. So nice to see you again." Turning away from Mary with some difficulty, Morris asked, "Air Vice-Marshal, how can I be of service to you?"

"I am very glad to have met you but I believe my task here is completed and I should return to my office." With that the air vice-marshal winked at his daughter, abruptly shook Morris's hand, and quickly exited the hotel. Morris was left facing Mary, who seemed not at all embarrassed by what had just transpired. She just stood there with a slight tilt to her head looking directly at Morris.

"I think I need a coffee," he stammered. "Why don't we go into the lounge."

Mary, with a slight frown, whispered, "Don't you think we should go upstairs?" She took his arm and guided him into the lift. After a long silence she asked for the fourth floor, Morris having been rendered speechless by everything that was happening. Although she was standing a good foot away from him, Morris felt the force of her being there. Not the heat or electricity or magnetism that one reads about, but an enveloping presence. As they exited the lift, Mary, as if reading his mind about what the lift operator must be thinking, said, "This is the Connaught, after all, and there is a war on."

Once in his room he could barely stand. Mary put a finger to her mouth and made a soft shushing sound, walked to the bed, and reaching behind the night table, unplugged a thick lamp cord.

"Now, are you going to kiss me or do I have to do absolutely everything?"

There was nothing hesitant about their embrace and although their lips met ever so gently the power of what was happening was clear to both of them. It was a kiss Morris knew he would remember for all of his days.

"I think I would like the cup of coffee now. I believe

I'm suddenly feeling a little, no a lot, less brave. Would you mind very much calling down for coffee?"

Morris, hesitant to let go of Mary, still holding her hand, reached for the phone.

"How may we be of service, Colonel Davidson?"

"I would like some coffee sent to my room please."

Morris had not taken his eyes off Mary as, still attached to him, she closed her eyes for a moment.

"Will that be coffee for two, sir?" Apparently news travelled fast at the Connaught.

After Morris had ordered coffee for two and hung up the phone he guided Mary across the room and holding both her hands sat her down in one of two matching armchairs. Gently touching her shoulder he said, "I think we need to talk about all this." Mary nodded and looked up at him, tears running down her cheeks. "I know, I tried so hard and now I am afraid of everything, afraid of what I have done and what I had come to believe." Kneeling down beside her and taking both her hands again, he said, "In this room, with me, you have nothing to be afraid of. Especially what you have come to believe. That is something to hold close, that is something to keep alive."

The coffee arrived on a rolling cart with a silver service and fine china. Morris dismissed the waiter, explaining that he would serve. He poured the coffee and sat across from Mary in the other armchair.

"Now, my sweet Mary, should I quote my boss? "The only thing we have to...'"

"No, please stop. I only want to hear your thoughts. I need to know what you think, no, what you feel. Please. I am so afraid of what you will say."

"I think you are magnificent. From the moment you first spoke to me at the airfield I have thought so. I am a logical man and I have not had a logical thought about you since then. When my mind is not focused on my work there is Mary. And sometimes she appears when I least expect her. And to be perfectly honest I have to push you away. Push you out of my thoughts. As you may imagine I have so much to do here and it is of such importance that I must be made of iron. But my darling I am not made of iron, and I am a failure at pushing thoughts of you away. So my solution, my logical solution, which has just come to me this moment, is to embrace you if you will have me."

Mary stood, and looking down at him, said, "I have so much to say to you, so much I want to tell you but for now I can only try to be your woman of iron and send you on your way." Mary shushed Morris again, walked to the bed, reinserted the lamp cord, and without another word gave him a salute and left the room.

It was almost afternoon by the time Morris arrived at the embassy. Bill Sherman was waiting for him with the now familiar Air Vice-Marshal Forrest-Wainwright.

"Morris, the air vice-marshal was telling me that you had a most interesting meeting this morning. I know you couldn't discuss the dark secrets we carry but at least you got to be acquainted with each other.

Before we get to work, tell me how that fine boy of yours is doing."

Morris paused before answering. It was unclear to him if what Willie Sherman was saying and asking had multiple meanings. This would have to be resolved. The truth, whatever it was, would have to be revealed to Willie. If the three of them were to work together Willie would have to know at least what Mary's father knew and the air vice-marshal would have to know more about Morris. He should not allow more secrets than absolutely necessary to interfere with their mission. It was a complex web already with Morris knowing things Willie was not privy to and Willie and Morris together having information they could not share with the air vice-marshal and god knows what the air vice-marshal was keeping from them.

"I think David is doing just fine. Thank you for asking."

Sherman turned to the air vice-marshal and said, "Morris' son David is a great lad, a particular favorite of the president. Having lost his mother so long ago he has the good fortune of having a wonderful grandmother to take care of him while his father is doing the nation's business."

Morris' only thought was, "Thank you, Willie, thank you, my friend."

Sherman, leading the way, said, "Let's move on to more secure quarters. Air Vice-Marshal, may I call you George? We Yanks tend to be more informal and if we're going to have heated disagreements I believe it takes the edge off and allows us to be less circumspect."

In the lower basement of the embassy at the end of a long musty yellow hallway with pipes running along the walls was a heavy steel door guarded by a marine corporal. Inside was a conference table, twelve chairs, and a crank operated field telephone. The air was damp and musty but a loud ventilation fan made it just bearable.

Sherman, making a point not to imply authority and sit down at the head of the table, gestured for them to take seats wherever they wanted and said, "This is the safest room in the house, I think we should brief each other on the latest developments. George, why don't you start before the mildew sets in."

"Thank you, William."

"Willie will be just fine. I think we're going to become good friends in this room."

"Then Willie it will be. As you know, my charge has been upgrading the Royal Air Force. In order to do that, I needed to procure the latest intelligence on aircraft development in Germany. Concomitant to that was the development of aircraft ordnance. Cannon, machine guns, and of course bombs. The boasts coming out of Germany, partially confirmed by whispers, suggest a new secret weapon in the early stages of development. This and reports of an ultrafast aircraft to deliver this weapon brought me to the prime minister, where I received limited confirmation of some of my intelligence and was informed there was more untold.

"Apparently, we three have been charged similarly, both by your president and by my prime minister. We are without portfolio, in truth we are without license. The consequence of imprisonment is not out of the question. You two gentleman are suspected of having already crossed the line of chargeable offenses. But that is history. History never to be revealed. Now, if we can get our names figured out we can proceed. Colonel Davidson, you are Morris Gold, barrister from New York, confidant of the American president, are you not?"

"Yes, of course, I was coming to that. Please call me Morris."

Willie Sherman stood up and started circling the table, reversing his direction whenever he passed the door.

"We have substantial information on the development of this new weapon, which we will of course share with you after you finish, but the ultrafast aircraft is new to us."

"Apparently the Germans are developing aircraft engines that use the force of burning fuel in a gas turbine internal combustion engine, rather than attaching an internal combustion engine to a propeller, to supply enough thrust to get an aircraft airborne and move it along at extremely high speeds. As you may understand, the dynamics of an airplane propeller, much like a ship's prop, by its very nature causes a limitation on maximum speed. At a certain point additional RPMs add nothing to the speed of the aircraft. In the simplest terms, although the propellers drive the aircraft they are also simply in the way. We have been working on these jet engines for some time. Our difficulty is getting them to maintain a slow enough speed. The cause of this is..."

"George, I think you've given us enough of the technical information, but surely the Germans currently have a bomber capable of delivering this weapon. What about the Junkers? It..."

"Of course the Germans are also working on a self-propelled rocket bomb, code named Cherrystone, but we don't think this flying bomb would have the capacity to carry very heavy ordnance. As for their bombers, although they have the capacity, they don't have the speed required to evade our fighter planes. These weapons, if successfully developed, will be both extremely heavy and scarce. It would be too high a risk to send one in a lumbering bomber which might..."

Interrupting, Morris asked, "So, do we stop the bomb or stop the bomber?"

"There is one more factor of particular interest to the two of you. It has been speculated that if the new engine is developed, an aircraft fitted with four such engines could cross the Atlantic with a large payload. Please understand this is conjecture and not based on research or intelligence."

"Did that little ditty come directly from the PM?" Sherman asked. "If so, it is totally unnecessary, we don't need any more incentive than we already have."

"It did come from the PM, but as you will note I have called it speculation and conjecture. I believe it is the PM's speculation and conjecture. There's more than one way to follow orders."

With that Willie said, "Now I know we're all going to get along."

Morris leaned forward on the table and looked directly at Willie. "I think this may be the time to read George into everything we know." Sherman stopped pacing, gave a slight nod, and sat down at the table.

"George, I know you have the PM's full trust and we, with good reason, do not. We three must come to an understanding, an agreement, an inviolable pact of secrecy. We may need not only to protect our bosses from knowledge of some decisions we will make and actions we may take. We may also decide among ourselves to go against their wishes. We must be able to resolve disputes between them among ourselves even if they are unable to do so. We can't depend on politicians who view their own tenure as the greater good. In the final analysis we can only trust each other." Sherman first turned to Morris and then to the air vice-marshal. "Are we all agreed on this?" Both nodded their consent.

Morris began by reviewing his meeting with Professor Einstein and the potential of the new bomb. He went on to reveal the information received from Rudolph Hess on the progress of the German bomb and to explain the efforts of the Americans to develop a super-bomb.

"It appears to me," Morris added, "that we three have no ability to advance the development of our bomb. That's in the hands of scientists, but we can interfere with Germany's progress on theirs. George, what is our capability of stopping this ultra-aircraft if we fail to stop the bomb?"

"Far from a sure thing, we can do massive bombing of where we believe the aircraft development sites are located. But we cannot be sure of success as our intelligence is not absolute and the targets not obvious. Of course we have a chance of shooting it down, but that is far from a certainty. Our latest Spitfire is very fast but maybe not fast enough. I believe we should make every effort to delay development of both the bomb and the ultra-aircraft through bombing and sabotage. But we cannot have confidence in the results."

Willie then added, "Even if we did stop the aircraft development the Germans could deliver the bomb on a sacrificial ship, a submarine that could sneak into any major harbor here or on the American coast. It's the bomb we must focus on. Lets not spend resources or our time on anything else. We must stop the bomb. What about Uncle Joe? He claims to have someone on the inside. Any chance of getting help on that front?"

"Not if we ask the PM," George answered, "He detests the man and his government. He mistrusts everything about him and has specifically ordered me not to involve the Soviets in any way. If we decide to approach the Russians we must keep it from him."

"And from FDR," Morris added. "I can try to connect with Litvinov. I can use connections that are outside normal channels; other connections."

"Be careful, my friend, it borders on trea—"

"No, not treason, worse. Using my mother-in-law."

Morris briefly explained the relationship between his late wife's mother and Litvinov's wife.

"Morris, I believe it's time for you to visit your son and his grandmother in New York. A family trip to Washington might also be in order. I'm sure lunch between two old friends would not be inappropriate. And you could take David to visit the old man himself."

The plan was simple. Morris' mother-in-law, Sarah, would arrange a small dinner party in New York for old friends: the Litvinov's, Susan and Harpo Marx, and, of course Morris, as Sarah's escort. Morris would approach Litvinov with the idea of collaboration and with the understanding that anything said would go back to Moscow. Litvinov was to believe that this was a sanctioned approach with both Churchill's and FDR's approval.

George picked up the field telephone handset

and cranked vigorously. "This is Forrest-Wainwright. Would you patch me to RAF seventeen please." After a lot of back and forth, code words, and many pauses, "Right then. Confirmed."

George, turning to both men, said, "I have Colonel Davidson on an RCAF return flight tomorrow at 1800."

Morris' cross-Atlantic flight, landing first in Iceland, then in Greenland, Labrador, and Newfoundland, took twenty-eight hours. Willie Sherman and the air vice-marshal stayed in London to work on alternative plans in the event that Morris' approach to Litvinov was unsuccessful.

GRAND CENTRAL STATION
NEW YORK CITY
OCTOBER 29, 1941

When Morris finally arrived in New York he was not surprised to see his son and his mother-in-law waiting for him at Grand Central Station. He had cabled ahead from Montreal. David, who was twelve, strode up to his father with outstretched hand. "Welcome home, Dad. Grandma really missed you."

"Well, I missed her too," Morris replied. "How's school?"

"We're studying the Crusades, and my chess game has improved. Math and English are easy but Hunter has no sports. It's as if they believe smart kids can't play anything but chess."

David was now attending a new elementary school for gifted children. It was a change instituted by his grandmother. This was her only grandson and she viewed him as her daughter's gift to the world. The devastation of Ruth's death was only made tolerable by having the chore of caring for her only grandchild, her precious David. Although she understood the importance—if not the reason—for Morris' many absences, she knew the hardship it was for a motherless boy not to have very much time with his father. In some ways though, she was actually grateful, as it gave her a major role in David's life. Both grandparent and surrogate parent.

Not that Sarah didn't have a full life otherwise. She was involved in the Zionist movement and active in rescue programs for the Jews trapped in occupied Europe. She had a full schedule of dinners, theatre, concerts, and the opera. Sarah was a true New Yorker, having been born and grown up in Greenwich Village, with many friends, most, but not all of whom, shared her political beliefs, were passionate supporters of this president and were apathetic about nothing. Truly a woman to be taken seriously.

On Morris' first morning home he took David to the newsreels on Seventy-second Street and then Barney Greengrass for lunch. The headline story was the sinking of the destroyer *Ruben James* with the loss of a hundred American sailors. It was the first sinking of a U.S. warship and Morris believed it would help FDR get public support for entering the war.

Walking home along Broadway David wondered aloud what it must be like to be on a sinking ship. "What does it feel like to drown, to be in a war, to have other people trying to kill you?"

"I think those questions can only be answered by someone who has survived those experiences. And I believe it may be different for each individual. I have met many people who have experienced combat in one form or another but I've always thought it would be an invasion of their privacy to ask them about it.

I recently met a British officer who was awarded the Victoria Cross. That's the highest—"

"I know," David interrupted, "it's like the Congressional Medal of Honor."

"That's right. Clearly he performed some heroic act, but I would never think of asking him about it. Maybe no explanation can suffice. Only those who experience combat can understand."

"Maybe they can talk to each other about it," David suggested.

"Yes, maybe they can."

The rest of the walk was in silence. Crossing Eighty-sixth Street Morris took his son's hand. He was thinking of David's mother and her courage and how so many lives had been changed by that single event.

That evening, after dinner and when David had gone to do his homework, Morris broached the all-important question to Sarah.

"Would you be willing to have lunch with Ivy Litvinov and arrange for a dinner party here in New York with Max and Ivy, Susan and Harpo, and the two of us? We could take David to Washington and I could take him to visit the White House while you had lunch with Ivy."

"You appear to have this already well planned. Is there more I should know about this proposed dinner party?"

"In this instance, Sarah, the less you know the better. I have no desire to see David's grandmother in violation of any laws. I can tell you, however," Morris lied, "that the president will appreciate your help."

"Of course I will help. Can I assume that you need some time alone with Max Litvinov?"

"About an hour should do."

"I believe I have a better idea, a public place with privacy. On Saturday the sixth of December, the Metropolitan Opera will be performing Wagner's *Die Walküre*. I was not planning to go but it seems appropriate for whatever you and Max are up to, and for Harpo it will be a real night at the opera. I'm sure we can use my friend Margery's box as Allen can't tolerate Wagner. I'll seat the two of you in the back row. Act Two should give you enough time to slip into the anteroom and get back to your seats under the cover of darkness before it's over. But I may have to tell Susan and Harpo something to get them to sit through five hours of Wagner."

"Tell them you'll be getting a terrible headache after Act Two. I'm sure Harpo will understand."

"That may just be the truth."

"Sarah, I knew you would help, but I had no idea how crafty you could be."

"I'm a mother and a grandmother, of course I am."

WASHINGTON, D.C.
NOVEMBER 8, 1941

The following Saturday, Morris, Sarah, and David took the late train from Pennsylvania Station to Washington. The plan was for Sarah to have lunch with Ivy Litvinov while David and his father visited the White House. David was too excited to sleep and spent most of the time talking about his most recent visit to the White House. When the train stopped in Baltimore, two military policemen boarded looking for Morris. The president was in Warm Springs and would not return to the White House until Monday. Morris was to accompany them to Annapolis for a meeting with James Forrestal, the undersecretary of the navy.

"You and David should continue on to Washington. I'm sorry I won't be there, but David, you should go with your grandmother and visit the Soviet embassy. I'm sure the ambassador's wife can arrange a grand tour for you while they have their luncheon. I'll join you tonight or tomorrow."

"OK, Dad, but do you think I should write a report for the president about what I see. I know they're our allies, but they haven't always been."

"No, David, I think you should be the perfect guest and not snoop around. These are our friends, especially the ambassador and Mrs. Litvinov."

After leaving the train in Baltimore, Morris was escorted to a waiting car and driven to the naval academy in Annapolis. The two closed-mouth MPs sat in the front seat and Morris took the silence as an opportunity to review the whole operation. Slightly dozing off, his thoughts then went to Mary and their time together at the Connaught. The thoughts seemed to attack him from all directions. Was this something to be stopped, was he being selfish? It was intrinsically unfair. Was he just a middle-aged man leading on a beautiful young woman infatuated with him? Was it just a salve for his loneliness, was he compromising his mission, what about David? But she was more than a beautiful young woman; she truly had captivated him, had taken a place in his very being.

He was willing to make sacrifices for his country and his son but he felt a need to have Mary in his life. Like never before. Morris also made the painful admission to himself that as much as he thought he loved David's mother, and he truly did love her fading memory, his feelings for Mary were different, far more powerful than anything he had felt in the past.

"Mr. Gold, sir, we've arrived. The guard at the gate will need your identification."

Morris rolled down his window and gave the guard his government ID. Returning it, the guard directed them to the commandant's quarters, where a well-decorated chief petty officer was waiting for him.

"Mr. Gold, the secretary is expecting you. If you will follow me."

They walked along a perfectly groomed winding path to the back of the building and entered a rear door. Forrestal, sitting at the kitchen table with a cup of coffee, half stood and gestured Morris to sit down across from him.

"The president, who is still in Warm Springs, has instructed me to update you on recent events." Looking down at an open file he continued, "You are of the Jewish race are you not, and your ancestry is either German or Russian if I am correct?"

"Mr. Secretary, I am adviser to the president of the United States, your commander in chief. He has instructed you to brief me. I strongly recommend that you proceed without sharing your thinly veiled personal questions of my loyalty."

Without looking up Forrestal continued.

"As of eighteen hundred hours Thursday we have been intercepting recurrent coded radio transmissions from the Imperial Japanese Navy headquarters to ships at sea. The location of these ships is unknown. The code has yet to be deciphered. It is the opinion of the Joint Planning Committee that some minor attack, blockade, or interference of American interests is imminent. When this occurs we are to respond with military force of equal measure. That is all."

Morris stood and left the building. He had no

intention of having a dialogue with the undersecretary. Outside, Morris looked up at the academy chapel dome with its Christian cross and thought, "Like it or not, Mr. Secretary, we are all in this together. We're going to war with the Japanese, and their allies, the Germans."

There was no car waiting for him. Morris pulled his collar up against the wind and walked toward the gatehouse. Not wanting any involvement with Forrestal or his cronies he had the guard telephone for a taxi.

The Annapolis town taxi was an aging DeSoto, and after being offered a five dollar tip the cabbie agreed to drive him the forty miles to Washington.

Aside from some minimal conversation with the driver and some hard bumps to the taxi's failing springs, the trip was uneventful. It gave Morris time to consider the brief meeting he had just had. Forrestal's attitude had not been unexpected. His anti-Semitism was not unknown to members of the Jewish community, especially those in government, but the discourtesy and disrespect had crossed the line. If the undersecretary had no desire to socialize or do business with Jews, that was his right, but the business of government was another matter. If his prejudice was going to interfere with that then he could only be a hindrance.

Even though he was unaware of Morris' relationship with the president or the task FDR had assigned to him, he had behaved in a way that would preclude any trust. Morris had seen in the past that bigotry could be stronger than and often confused with patriotism. The undersecretary could never be made aware of the actions of Morris and Willie Sherman. The risk to the operation as well as to the participants was too high.

When war came the country was going to change. All Americans would have to participate in some way, Catholics and Negroes, women and children, and yes, even Jews. People like Forrestal and Lindbergh would never change, but they would have to keep their intolerance among themselves.

When Morris arrived at the Hay-Adams hotel he found his son and mother-in-law sitting in the lobby with Ivy Litvinov. When they saw Morris their animated conversation stopped. Apparently there was some subject or plot that was not to be shared with him. The last time Ivy and Sarah had gotten together they had made a list of women who might make a good stepmother for David, but he couldn't imagine they would involve David in that particular discussion.

"You all seem to be enjoying yourselves. David, how was your visit to the embassy?"

"I had lunch with Alina Gerasimova and her mother. Did you know that they eat the same food as you do at Barney Greengrass? I ate some herring to be polite but I still find it—I still don't like it. Alina is a little older than I am and speaks English perfectly. I was a little ashamed that I don't know any Russian. But she invited me to visit the consulate in New York, where she will teach me some Russian."

Ivy turned to Sarah and shook her head slightly, indicating that this would not be a good idea.

"I see you have a red star lapel pin," Morris said.

"It was a gift from Alina's mother, she pinned it on my jacket. I guess I should take it off now." Sarah reached over, unfastened the pin, and slipped it into her pocketbook.

"I'll keep that for David. Our lunch was here in the hotel and we had so much to talk about that we ran out of time. So Max and Ivy are coming to New York to join us for dinner and the opera on the sixth, and we're inviting Susan and Harpo as well."

"Sounds like a festive evening. What opera are we hearing?"

"Wagner's *Die Walküre*."

"Well, at least dinner will be enjoyable."

The next morning Morris and David had an early breakfast together while Sarah packed for the return trip to New York.

"Dad, Grandma and Mrs. Litvinov think you have a girlfriend."

Morris now understood the secret conversation he had interrupted.

"What makes them think that?"

"Well, Grandma says you are standing up much straighter, and you are looking younger, and she says she just knows these things."

"Did she ask you how you felt about this?"

"You know Grandma. She told me how I felt."

"Was she right?"

"Mostly right."

"Are you going to tell me, or is it a secret?"

"Well, I wouldn't mind if it was someone I liked and she was as pretty as Alina."

Looking at his watch Morris said, "Grandma should be finished packing by now, so let's go upstairs and get our suitcases."

"Well, do you?"

"I don't know, David, but when I do you will be the first to know."

NEW YORK CITY
DECEMBER 6, 1941

It was opera night and after dinner at Cavanagh's, the old steak house on West Twenty-third Street, Max had the consulate limousine take all six of them to the opera house on Thirty-ninth and Broadway. As expected, the ride was punctuated by Max and Harpo keeping up a stream of not so subtle old jokes. Both of them seemed to get as much pleasure out of these as if they were being told for the first time. Almost everyone in the car had heard them many times before. This didn't matter as the laughter of the two men was so infectious that with the exception of the stern-faced driver everyone was hysterical for most of the ride.

The box at the opera house consisted of two areas. The front box overlooking the stage had eight chairs, the rear two chairs being higher than the others so patrons could see the stage. Behind the box area was a separate sitting room, or anteroom, with a chaise and a coat rack.

The opera went as planned. At the beginning of the second act, after the house lights had come down, Morris motioned for Max to follow him into the anteroom at the rear of the box. They sat together on the chaise while Morris explained his request, in a muted voice just loud enough to hear over the music.

"Max, I assume you realized that this was more than a social evening."

"Of course. The choice, the operatic selection, revealed that. Who would choose Wagner? Please understand that even as ambassador I am watched all the time. It is the Russian nature of searching for treachery. And often it's discovered even when it's not really there."

"I will be exceedingly brief. I am responding to the information that you conveyed to Secretary of State Hull. I fully expect and desire that you report this meeting to Premier Stalin as the request comes from the highest levels in our government. We are requesting direct communication with your infiltrator of German weapons development. As you may know, our own scientists are progressing at a rapid rate, but we would be more comfortable knowing the exact degree of German progress as we believe they may have a substantial lead over us. I don't know what assurances your government will require from us, so please view this as the opening to further discussions. I must, however, stress the urgency of this as the weapon could be used on multiple fronts."

"I will of course convey your request by cable on my return to Washington."

Max leaned forward and in an even quieter voice said, "You must keep David away from Alina Gerasimova. That woman is not her mother."

The next day the world changed.

Lies of War

NEW YORK CITY
DECEMBER 7, 1941

After reading the news and completing the cross-word puzzle Morris sat in his living room overlooking the Hudson river. On a yellow legal pad he outlined the events of the past few weeks. These notes, along with others already locked in a safe deposit box, were intended to be an accurate record of his activities. He believed that history should eventually reflect the truth or nothing useful could be learned from it. How long it would be before these notes could or would be revealed was unknown to him, but the very existence of them was imperative. Maybe if the true history of past wars—not the self-serving memoirs of kings and generals, not the redacted secrets of governments and collaborations—were revealed, the very nature of conflict would change. Possibly war would become less frequent and national leaders would try to avoid what was now considered inevitable. After a short break for lunch he returned to his notes, trying to justify the collusion between himself, Willie, and George.

"Dad, come listen to the radio. The Japanese are bombing Hawaii. Hurry up!"

In the kitchen David and his grandmother were standing around the radio listening to an unclear report. They had just tuned into the *Round Table* from the University of Chicago on the NBC Red Network. The statement from the president's press secretary, Steve Early, was brief. "The Japs have attacked Pearl Harbor, all military activities on Oahu Island." The news announcer was trying to explain where Oahu Island was in relation to the mainland. More reports of other attacks kept being announced. It later turned out that many of these reports were false. The Philippines and Burma had not been attacked.

Morris knew that as catastrophic as this attack might turn out to be, it also, at last, brought the United States fully into the war. It did not appear to be the minor action predicted by Forrestal and the Joint Planning Committee but a major attack on the Pacific fleet. The telephone lines to Washington were unavailable and knowing that it would be impossible to speak with anyone in his own government, as all thoughts would be on Japan, he called the British consulate in New York and arranged for an urgent cable to George in London. After spending the afternoon in discussion with David and Sarah about what this attack meant for the country and for them as a family, Morris received a messenger at his door, not from the British consulate but from the War Department, with orders for Colonel Davidson to report to Naval Air Station Floyd Bennett Field. Willie and George had done their magic and gotten him a priority flight on this impossible day.

At the air station a PBY with RAF markings was waiting for him. The amphibious patrol plane was part of the government's lend-lease program and had been scheduled to be overhauled and updated with new and more powerful engines before returning to service. Morris was reassured that the Old Bird, as she was named, still had enough life to make the crossing.

"If the engines don't make it all the way she still floats and someone might pick you up before she sinks. Lots of U-boat crews out there who would love to capture an American colonel. First Yank POW." This was from the cheerful RAF mechanic who had come over on her the prior week.

"She'll make it. I'll bet your life on it, Colonel."

With an air speed of not much over 125 miles per hour, plus fueling stops, the Old Bird reached the English coastline almost forty hours later. After arranging transportation to London, Morris showered in the officers' quarters and tried to telephone Willie at the embassy. Apparently Air Vice-Marshal Forrest-Wainwright and attaché William Sherman had gone shooting for the day and would not be available until the evening. Glad that his two colleagues were getting on so well Morris took the opportunity to sleep. He slept in the car to London and once in his rooms at the Connaught he slept again.

The flight had been unbearable. Between the constant roar of the engine, the rattle and vibration of the fuselage and the turbulence he had not slept more than ten contiguous minutes. He would fall asleep only to have a bounce or change in engine pitch wake him. The pilot was on the lookout for German ships or U-boats he could report back to his base about, and would descend to almost wave top level to check what might be a periscope or snorkel.

When they spotted convoys headed to England they kept their altitude so as not to unnerve the crews or get shot down in error. There was no radio communication with the ships as that would have allowed the Germans to triangulate on their position and have U-boat wolf packs intercept them. Morris realized that being a merchant seaman in the North Atlantic was far more dangerous than flying in a rattling PBY. He was reminded of his conversation with David about the sinking of the *Ruben James*. These sailors were courageous in peacetime but in wartime being constantly on the alert for enemy submarines and aircraft, with the risk of sinking increased a hundredfold, their courage was remarkable.

LONDON
DECEMBER 10, 1941

Morris had no idea how to reach Mary discreetly. He
certainly didn't want to ask the embassy to locate her
or go through her command. There was no reasonable explanation he could give as to why he wanted
this particular driver except that he believed he was
in love with her. He decided to walk to the embassy.
For American Colonel Davidson the typically reserved
population of London had changed. Men in bowler
hats greeted him on the street with a nod, taxi drivers waved from their cars with a, "Welcome, Yank,"
and the stoic bobby outside the hotel actually saluted
him. When he passed a bombed site being cleared the
workers started singing, "the Yanks are coming." The
British, being the last European holdout against Hitler and having been battered by the Japanese in the
Far East, knew that their chance of survival depended
on the Americans entering the war and now the Yanks
had no choice.

Although not easily embarrassed, Morris felt
uncomfortable; he believed the aid from the United
States should have come much sooner. FDR had done
all he could with a resistant congress but as a nation it
had disappointed its longtime ally. Walking the streets
he passed beautiful townhouses followed by bombed

out ruins; it was the randomness of the blitz, what had been spared and what had been destroyed, that struck him. Reminded again of the convoy sailors always vulnerable to attack. All Londoners, and actually all British, were under the same cloud, not knowing who would live and who would die.

When he reached Grosvenor Square he could see the embassy building surrounded by huts, which served the crew for a blimp that was stationed there. Willie had told him that the blimp, nicknamed Romeo, was manned by women of the WAAF and was used for early detection of German bombers. As he approached the embassy itself there was an obvious increase in security. Bobbies and Home Guard troops surrounding the building, with U.S. Marines outside the front entrance. Morris walked around to the staff entrance and after being saluted by the Marine guard and having his military identification checked, he was asked who had won the world series that year and how many stars were on the first American flag. Thanks to David he knew the answer to the first question.

The attack on Pearl Harbor had caused a change. The embassy was bustling with activity, apparently far more American military personnel had been stationed in London than had been made public. Uniformed officers of both the Army and Navy were everywhere. Desks and chairs were being set up in the hallways, and social rooms were being converted into offices. Handwritten signs were posted with organizational names and arrows directing people to their assigned places. The basement room, however, was intact, with a familiar Marine guard standing at the door, only now he was armed. "Colonel Davidson, the others have just arrived."

Inside, Willie and George were in animated conversation. In front of Willie was a shiny .45 caliber pistol in a new holster, which he pushed towards Morris.

"I signed this out for you. Don't lose it or I will have to pay for it."

"I thought you and George were in the country shooting."

"Actually we were in the lower basement taking target practice. Welcome back. Successful mission?"

Morris took off his coat and sat down as far away from the pistol as he could.

"All went as planned until the Japanese attack. I believe Litvinov will get the message to Stalin and we'll be able to negotiate some access to their inside man. Max seemed all for it but he was in no position to commit to anything. With us now in the war the Russians may be more inclined to help. I also met with Forrestal. I think his standing may fall after this attack. His and the joint committee's assessment was far off the mark. I believe the president would have acted differently had he known the scope of what the Japanese were up to. George, any progress here?"

"We have increased our raids on Brest and are getting more intelligence through radio intercepts about the ultra-aircraft development. We have increased our raids on Vemork in Norway. Norsk Hydro is producing something called heavy water, which is used in the production of the super-bomb. As you might expect it is very heavily defended and a tricky bomb run. Our losses are high, so convincing the high command of the importance of something they don't understand required the PM to issue a direct order. We believe we have destroyed some of their stockpile but really cannot be sure.

"Eventually we will need a commando raid with the help of the Norwegian underground and, once the United States is fully in the fray, with more bombers, we will be better equipped to prepare for the raid. Although your president has not declared war on Germany yet, we are assuming it will happen shortly. His speech was moving and I understand all Americans' thoughts are on the Japanese attack. But surely declaring war with Germany is inevitable."

Willie interrupted. "I don't think the boss is going to declare war on Germany. That would require his asking for an act of congress. There are those in congress who are isolationists and those who think that a second front, Europe, would be untenable, as well as those who still don't accept the true evil of Herr Hitler. You also should understand American politics. To many of the opposition party, the Republicans, defeating FDR and his social programs is more important than the defense of England. He'll wait for Germany to declare against the United States. Because of their alliance with Japan that will happen soon, within the week I believe, and congress will be forced to declare a state of war."

"Are you saying that the populace of your country doesn't understand the consequences of what is happening here and the risk to our very civilization? That they're against fighting to protect it? Have I overestimated the intelligence of the American people?"

"We are a young country, George; we need time to mature. We lost over a hundred thousand men in the last war and over two hundred thousand were wounded. Nearly every American family was affected and all this without threat to our homeland. Many wonder why. Only twenty percent support entering the war in Europe. I'm sure that will change, and may have already, but the president is a consummate politician and knows when to be patient and when to act. We'll be in it by the end of the week."

"May your words be true, Willie."

"Amen. If my meeting with Max Litvinov produces the result I expect we shouldn't have to wait very long for an answer to what the Russians want in exchange. I imagine some negotiation will be required, but in the end we'll get what we need without giving up all of eastern Europe. Until then all we can do is keep up the pressure on German bomb and aircraft development."

"Morris, let's not forget that Europe is not ours to give up."

"Not yet, anyway."

With that Willie slid the .45 to Morris and said, "This meeting is adjourned. Take the gun and get some practice in."

As they prepared to leave, George caught Morris' arm and asked for a private moment.

"Morris, Mary's happiness is very important to me. After her mother died she fell into a spell of depression, that is until now. She appears to be her old self again. I don't want that to change. I don't want her hurt. If your feelings for her may be transient or not serious I implore you to clarify it with her now before she becomes even more involved with you. I know this may be an inappropriate request as she is an adult, but I am still her father and thus very protective of her. I like you and have come to trust you so I believe you will do the right thing."

"George, I want you to know—"

"Don't answer me, just do what is right."

"How do I find her?"

"I imagine she is parked outside your hotel. I told her you would be returning today."

Morris chose to take the time to walk back to his hotel in spite of the cold drizzle. He tried to consider the possibility that he was merely infatuated with Mary; that this was an impossible relationship not to be continued. If it continued, would he break her heart later? Would his life take over and leave no room for her? He had a family and a life in New York. This war would eventually end and he would in all probability return to that life. He barely knew her and he didn't want to hurt her. By the time he arrived at the Connaught he had made a decision. As much as he thought he wanted to be with her, he had to protect her from himself. He had to explain how it must end before it really started. How he truly liked her but there was no chance of them being together.

There she was standing in the cold next to the drophead coupe.

"If it isn't Colonel Davidson."

Morris, not putting his arm around her, said, "Mary, you must be freezing, come inside with me. Your father told me you might be here waiting for me."

"I can't believe he told you that. What else did he tell you?"

"Basically that he loves you very much."

"I'm sure there was more."

"Yes, but let's get you warm."

Hesitating, Morris then said, "Come upstairs so you can dry off."

Once in the room his resolve was lost. Mary stood in front of him, unbuttoned and slipped off her uniform jacket. She was wearing what appeared to be a silk shirt, which clung lightly to the shape of her small breasts. Morris could see that she was not wearing any undergarment and her nipples were clearly defined.

This was a moment of dizzying proportions for him. A feeling of abandoning his past, a past that he cherished, a past that had produced his wonderful son, David, a past of focus and control. Without thinking he reached forward and began fumbling with the small pearl buttons on Mary's shirt.

"I think you should let me do this. You have very large hands."

"I'm not very steady at this."

"No, you're not, and if we're going to go to bed together any time soon I think I should move things along. But I imagine you are capable of undressing yourself."

"Yes, of course, at least I do know how to take my own clothes off."

"Well do get on with it," Mary laughed.

Standing facing each other surrounded by a floor covered in clothes, Mary reached between Morris' legs and held him for a moment. His penis grew rigid in her hand, and she quickly let go and stroked his cheek. Morris pulled her to him and holding her sides with both hands put his thumbs on her nipples. They too grew hard. This time their kiss was not as soft, their tongues met and explored each other's mouths. Morris moved his hand down to her thighs and reaching behind her gently lifted her against him. Mary wrapped her legs around him and kissed him as hard as she could.

"Take me to the bed, just take me, be inside me."

With an amazing feat of grace Morris set Mary down on the bed, knelt in front of her and with his mouth touched her face and her neck, lingered on her breasts and nipples, slid down to her stomach and eventually between her legs. He reached under her and lifted her to him. He felt her knees pressing harder and harder against the sides of his head. Then suddenly she grabbed him under his arms and pulled his mouth to hers.

"Now, oh please god, now."

Morris slid her fully onto the bed and using his hand guided himself into her. Although she was so wet he felt a firmness that caused him to hesitate.

"Do it my darling, just do it, be inside of me. Do it now."

Morris pushed himself in and lost all sense of himself, until he realized that their rhythm was quite different. Mary was moving much faster than he could possibly keep up. She was jazz and he was concerto.

"My darling, could we slow down a little? Can we try to move slowly? Maybe I'm not very good at this."

"You are perfect, I want you slowly. I want this to last forever." But in a few moments it was over, Mary and Morris reached the same place at the same time.

"Don't come out of me yet. Stay inside me as long as you can. Stay with me as long as you can."

After making love again, this time even more slowly, Mary said, "I am absolutely famished, darling. Can we get some supper?"

The only table available was near the kitchen doors, but they hardly noticed the waiter's comings and goings. They couldn't take their eyes off each other and talked without pause. To Morris it was miraculous how Mary knew his very thoughts as he spoke them. For Mary it was the same. He ordered a bottle of Bordeaux and Mary consumed both hers and Morris' bread portion almost immediately. It consisted of two very small rolls due to rationing. The entrée was a stew of vegetables and rabbit; again rationing and the war effort had restricted what even the finest restaurants could serve. Morris felt somewhat guilty about the bounty of food available to Americans.

Before the war Britain had imported most of its wheat and, of course, this was no longer obtainable. With more drink than food in his system he became slightly giddy, suddenly remembering the hidden microphone in his room. He must have become flushed in some way because Mary instantly understood and said, "Worry not, darling, I cut the wire ages ago. When you were abroad I explained that I was picking up some documents for you and went in and snipped them. No one noticed since no one is listening when you are not in residence."

"How did you know that was what—"

"I was quite curious as to how long it would take for you to remember. I certainly hope your government work is more efficient. What else did my father say to you?"

"He explained that he was an .accomplished swordsman with sabers, a crack shot, and quite willing to shoot—"

"He didn't!"

"No, of course not. He wanted me to be sure of my feelings for you. He didn't want you to be hurt."

"And are you?"

"Am I what?" asked Morris, staging a confused look on his face.

"Stop it. You're not being fair."

Morris looked across the table at Mary, and taking both of her hands in his, said, "I am sure. My only doubt is if I could possibly love you more than I do at this very moment. That is inconceivable to me."

"What do we do now?"

"We go upstairs, and then tomorrow morning we will both talk to your father before he hacks off my right arm."

"Darling, he really likes you. The most he would do is lop off your—"

'Don't say it."

"I was going to say your hand. What were you possibly thinking?"

LONDON
DECEMBER 11, 1941

The next morning, before they could speak to Mary's father, Morris received a note requesting his presence at the Finnish legation. This was clearly a message from the Russians as they shared the same building. Not wanting to make his embassy nor the British aware of the meeting, Morris put on civilian clothes and called on Willie to pick him up in a taxi. He had no intention of meeting the Russians alone. George would have to wait.

When they arrived for the meeting two burly Russians met them at the door, tried to separate them and maneuver Morris into the back of a waiting car. Willie would have none and of it and, while the two thugs were dealing with Morris, pushed his way into the front passenger seat. After some heated discussion in minimal English it was agreed that Willie was welcome to join them. After they relieved Willie of his .45—Morris of course was unarmed—the car proceeded to a not very elegant townhouse in Bayswater. It was surrounded by several bomb-damaged buildings but the street was not as damaged as other parts of London, which had been devastated. After being hustled up the steps and inside they were greeted by the smiling face of an obviously intoxicated Russian diplomat. Willie looked at his watch and then at Morris. It was ten o'clock in the morning.

"Come gentlemen, we have much to talk about. I hope you had a pleasant journey."

His English was quite correct, if stilted. At least they would be able to communicate. Willie and Morris followed him into a musty parlor with threadbare furniture. He beckoned them to sit on a stained settee barely wide enough for the two of them. Still standing, he said, "My name is unimportant, but you can call me Tommy if you wish. I am here to respond..." He took a crumpled piece of paper from his jacket pocket and looked at it intently, "...to Mr. Gold's request for the Union of Soviet Socialist Republics to give much needed assistance to the president of the United States."

It was clear that this was not going to be the high level meeting Morris had expected. Tommy was obviously in no position to negotiate on behalf of the Soviets. This was clearly the first step in what might become a too long process. Tommy then continued.

"I have been instructed by my government to proceed with confrontation on the matter at hand."

Hoping that he had actually intended to say cooperation or conversation, Morris smiled and nodded. The Russian then turned to one of the two thugs and snapped his fingers. A bottle of clear liquid, obviously vodka, appeared with three already filled glasses.

"Let us drink to our new friendship and may our

two homelands be harmonious."

It seemed to Morris that Tommy was trying out his English vocabulary with moderate success. Looking at his watch and then at Willie—it was now approaching eleven A.M.—Morris stood and said, "Yes, of course, a toast to the Soviet Socialist Republic and the United States of America." Willie stood and all three drank. Tommy immediately refilled the glasses.

"Now a drink to our glorious leaders."

Willie raised his glass and said, "To our leaders, za lyoo-bóf."

Tommy broke into a broad grin and said, "Da, za lyoo-bóf. To women."

Apparently Willie's Russian was not nearly as good as Tommy's English. But progress was being made and thankfully the drinking seemed to have come to an end. The three men sat, Morris and Willie squeezed on the settee and the Russian on a hard wooden chair. In a soft voice Willie said, half to himself, "I thought I was saying 'to your health.'"

"Now, down to business, as you Americans say. As we are soon to be true allied nations it is essential that we share the technology to defeat the German menace. We are most willing to provide you with information from our patriotic agent now courageously working within the Nazi weapons laboratory. And naturally you will welcome our own scientists to work along-side your own in the American and British weapons laboratories. In this way we can share our knowledge to defeat the Axis. It would be of great advantage if this arrangement could be consummated with all due haste. Although I am sanctioned to finalize this cooperation I am aware that you may require a more senior level of approval. I can expect that at our next meeting. Yes?"

Morris, knowing that this would not be possible with or without "more senior level of approval," realized that the gang of three, as they now referred to themselves, would have to figure out a way around this. The thought of giving the Russians access, of having Russian scientists on the inside, was unthinkable.

"We cannot speak for the British, of course. But we will convey this request to the proper parties within our government."

"I must assert that we require a direct presence in both American and British facilities. This is a most deliberate part of my instructions. If you cannot accomplish this we must use other channels to approach the British government, although that might be uncomfortable for your president as we do not believe he has been fully forthright with his friend Mr. Churchill."

Morris tried not to react. Tommy had just revealed that the Russians had access not only to communication between the PM and the president but also to progress on the bomb development program. Whether this was a slip-up or an intentional warning was not clear.

"We will certainly keep that in mind. Thank you

for meeting with us. If you will excuse us we must return to our embassy. How can we communicate our response?"

"I too must return. I know we will find a way to communicate with each other. We will drive you. Yes?"

Willie stood and said, "Thank you, but I think a walk would be best."

Tommy snapped his fingers twice and one of his men handed him a package. With a smile he gave it to Willie.

"This is a gift for you in the spirit of our friendship and to women."

Taking it, Willie could feel the shape of a bottle.

"Thank you, and may peace come to both our great countries."

Walking down the steps, Willie and Morris were silent, in fact they were silent until they were sure no one was in earshot.

"Did you hear that?"

"Willie, someone close to the president is giving information to the Soviets."

"Possibly. It could also be just a reasonable assessment and a bluff, or it could be someone in Churchill's circle who knows more than we think. If it is a spy, maybe we can take advantage of him with disinformation."

"Or a her; it could be a woman. Clever word disinformation."

Morris stepped up his pace and looking around said, "Lets find a pub where we can call the embassy to get us picked up. I don't see any taxis here."

In the now so very familiar basement room Morris and Willie briefed George on the Russian meeting.

"Nothing the Russians said to you is to be believed without verification. Tell me, what did you think of this Tommy fellow? It appears he must be someone of some experience or he wouldn't have been chosen for this mission. As you describe, he acted the way the Russians believe we think of them. Not without merit, we do undervalue their shrewdness particularly when they appear to be drunk, but I am confident that every word you spoke will be analyzed for its true hidden meaning. Putting you both close together on the settee made it possible for a microphone to hear both your voices and everything was probably written down by a listener in the next room.

"In spite of their disdain for our ability at analysis and subterfuge they still expect us to make some, even if ineffective, effort to mislead or misinform. To give, using Willie's word, disinformation. Thus, even your bad Russian language skills will be thought to possibly have some hidden meaning. Maybe your real intent was to mislead them into believing that we have a woman spy in the Kremlin or the complete opposite. Read the Russian writers, the convolutions and complications of thought are remarkable. It's how they keep warm in the winter, thinking and thinking and rethinking everything until the resulting rats' nest comes to an all too often incorrect conclusion. Even when trying to be honest and open, a Russian's resulting conclusion is so far from reality that it is usually wrong. You can't trust an honest Russian any more than you can trust a dishonest one."

Willie, smiling at George, said, "You appear to have the same view as your PM."

"Not really, he thinks they are barbarous, ignorant liars. I have a more generous view."

"If what you say is correct, Tommy may have wanted us to believe they have a spy in the White House or at Number Ten. Or, maybe he just made a mistake, a slip of the tongue."

"Morris, you have to understand the Russians don't make mistakes like that. Whoever Tommy is he is certainly not of a high enough level to know of an infiltrator of such importance. This information came to them some other way and is being used to put pressure on us and has the additional benefit of having us chasing our tails looking for a phantom nonexistent spy in our midst."

"If we accept that view, and I do, we're left with the real dilemma: do the Russians actually have an agent working in the German secret weapons laboratory or not? How do we verify or disprove their claim?"

Willie, no longer amused by George's view of the Russian character, said, "Make them prove it. It seems perfectly reasonable, and I'm sure the Russians expect this from us, that we request some form of proof: photographic or scientific evidence that we can confirm."

George nodded his agreement and Morris said, "I'm sure Tommy will contact me very soon, so let's prepare ourselves and have our counter-demands ready. No cooperation will be considered until we have verifiable proof of this agent's existence. To limit more demands on their part I propose we will tell them that this requirement comes directly from our superior, who does not believe a word of it, and has ordered us to participate in no further negotiation unless incontrovertible, irrefutable proof is provided. In other words, let's call their bluff. Is this some low level feint, or the real thing? We also should insist on knowing who we are dealing with. Who is Tommy?"

"Morris, I'm both impressed and concerned that you're beginning to think like a Russian."

"Willie, did you think my grandfather came over on the Mayflower with yours?"

"There is just one more item of business."

Handing the wrapped bottle to George, Willie said, "Would you have your people examine this and see if Tommy was trying to poison us or just get us drunk?"

As the "gang of three" prepared to leave, Morris turned to George. "Can you join me for dinner? I have a personal matter to discuss with you."

Before George could answer Willie said, "Don't forget your sidearm, you may need it. A father's wrath... Oh, never mind. Have a good dinner, boys."

"What exactly do you mean?"

"Really Morris, do you think the British, the Russians, and probably the Germans, are the only ones spying on you. I received a report on your driver from Army Signal Intelligence. Suffice it to say she is cleared of any suspicion. The remainder of the report should be of no concern to either of you as it has been destroyed in triplicate."

Morris and George met at a restaurant in Holborn. The ornate grill room was crowded with well-dressed customers. Both men, still in uniform, were seated in a corner away from other patrons. Now that Germany had just declared war on the United States it was understood that an American and a British officer of such high rank would appreciate privacy.

"Did you bring your gun?"

"I thought it unnecessary. Mary believes your choice of weapons would probably be sabers."

"That certainly would be traditional, but unfair. I don't believe the training at the Harvard School of Law is the same as at the Royal Military College. In any event we both appear to have the same interest in Mary's well-being. The only difference being that I am her father and well trained as a swordsman. I think we should leave this private table to a couple in need of it, and walk."

Morris left a few coins on the table and they walked out onto Kingsway. It was a cool but surprisingly dry evening and they set a leisurely pace.

After about a quarter mile Morris broke the silence.

"To get directly to your concerns, I really don't

know how to answer you. I can't predict the future so I'm left with a quandary. I am quite taken by your daughter, but the possible outcomes of life are complicated and unpredictable. I am some years older than Mary, I have a young son in the States who has never really known a mother, there is this awful war, and there is, of course, a cultural and religious difference that cannot be ignored. If it were solely my decision the honorable thing would be to distance myself from Mary and not subject her to the risk, the likelihood, of being hurt. But the decision is not mine alone, it's equally Mary's as well. I don't know the outcome but I do know I will do everything I can to allow Mary to make her decision. I can assure you that I will never deceive or mislead her. I know this is not a satisfactory answer for a concerned loving father, but it's the best I can provide. Do know that I care very much for your daughter."

"No, it is not enough of an answer. Not nearly enough. I see the joy she is feeling, a joy I have not seen in her since she was a child, but I dread the downfall should that be taken away from her. I want to know that you will be there to take care of her, that you will never hurt her. But that is an unreal expectation and if you had told me just that I would momentarily be relieved and happy for her, but it would be meaningless. You're asking me to trust you to be honest and to believe in Mary's ability to make her own choices, take her own risks. I'm glad to know you, Morris."

"And I to know you."

"I think now we should stop for something to eat before our follower thinks we're plotting something."

"You noticed the young man with the removable mustache," Morris said.

"A man in training, no doubt."

NEW YORK CITY
DECEMBER 22, 1941

Morris had spent only a short time in London, seeing Mary briefly, before returning to the States with George and the PM on the battleship HMS *Duke of York* arriving at Annapolis on December 22. The trip was so rough that even the PM, former First Lord of the Admiralty, claimed it to be "my longest week since the war began." While in the States, George spent several weeks in New York examining new aircraft at the Naval Air Station, Floyd Bennett Field in Brooklyn.

The first of the Douglas Boston light bombers originally ordered by France but now slated for Britain were on the field with RAF markings, ready for delivery. George wanted to determine how much additional training his pilots would require and what changes would need to be made to accommodate British armaments. The first and most obvious change was to switch the flight check lists from French to English. *Roues vers le basis* is not a fine French wine or a street in Paris but wheels down, and *volets rentrés* is flaps retracted. On one test flight, landing in South Carolina, the plane was surrounded by police and well-armed local residents who confused the RAF target emblem with the red circle on Japanese aircraft. After a few tense moments George was able to convince them that he was, in fact, British and not the enemy.

His primary mission was to coordinate forthcoming bombing strategy with his American counterparts, persuading them to focus on particular sites in Germany and occupied Europe. This, of course, had to be accomplished without revealing the true nature of the targets. In many cases the British would have to take the lead as the Americans found it difficult to risk their fliers' lives on seemingly, although well-defended, nonstrategic targets.

Morris spent much of the following months in New York and Washington with an occasional trip to Princeton to be briefed by Einstein on the significance of the reports being supplied by the Soviets. He exchanged letters with Mary on an almost daily basis. Of course with the war they could only write of the most mundane things. Plays seen, meals eaten, and the weather. But contained within these letters was an unwritten and clear intimacy.

On one trip Einstein became quite agitated by the thought that this new weapon might actually be used by either side. He believed that even men of conscience would resort to the bomb if, as he put it, "they believed their feet were to be in the flames." Morris had been so focused on stopping the Germans that he had not even considered the Allies using the bomb except as a threat by exploding it in some uninhabited, godforsaken place. If the Germans and the Japanese could actually see the damage of this weapon it would, in all probability, end the war. Even the Germans would be unwilling to inflict such horror on their own people. Einstein, however, had come to believe that if it was finally perfected, no nation could resist using it against its enemies, as in war, "one's feet are always in the flames."

PART II

Although in frequent contact through coded cables it was over a year before the "gang of three" were able to meet again. Willie had been coordinating the supply of information coming from the Russians with Robert Oppenheimer, who was heading up the U.S. bomb development. Morris had been in London, frequently meeting with Tommy, and George was in the States insuring the modification and delivery of aircraft to Britain. When they finally did meet again it was at George's townhouse in London.

LONDON
APRIL 13, 1943

His man had set out coffee, tea, and sandwiches without crust. This British habit always dismayed Morris who thought the outer crust was the best part of almost any bread.

Without any greeting Willie asked Morris, "And how is your friend Tommy doing?"

"He's actually quite an interesting fellow. Not so

unlike us in his attitude toward governmental leaders. I believe he is unequivocally unwilling to betray his country but will do his patriotic best to deceive his leaders when necessary."

"Is he to be trusted?" George asked.

"As long as our interests coincide, as long as Germany is a threat. After that I believe the Soviets will have other objectives in mind."

"Not anything the three of us can control. I'm afraid all we can do is stop this wretched bomb," Willie added.

The meeting went on for some hours, each of the three reporting on their various activities in great detail. Dinner, served in the library, was sausages and potatoes in individual crocks followed by cheese and port wine.

When the meeting finally broke up Morris stayed behind for a private conversation with George, who motioned for him to bring his glass and, carrying the decanter of port wine and his own glass, led Morris into his private study. It was a small room just off the library. The walls were covered with photographs of family. One that particularly caught Morris' eye was of a young Mary holding a trophy of some sort, but not smiling. George sat at his desk with Morris facing him in an overstuffed dark brown leather chair. After refilling their glasses Morris started.

"I need your advice on one matter."

George nodded.

"I must go to the States to brief the president and the PM in Washington on the eighteenth of next month. I want to ask Mary to join me and then travel to New York so I can introduce her to my son, David, and his grandmother. Do you have any suggestions on how I can inconspicuously accomplish this without violating any regulations or causing a scandal?"

"I will think this over. Mary has met the PM several times and I know she has charmed him because he almost always asks about her well-being. That girl appears to have an effect on older men... Oh, I'm so very sorry, I really wasn't meaning to include you in that group. I believe our friendship has caused me to be less circumspect in our conversations."

"George, this is a good thing, I value that about our friendship and of course I take no offense. But if you don't wish to assist this aging, decrepit lawyer, I'll understand."

"I will do what I can, young man."

RMS QUEEN MARY
MAY 5, 1943

When the RMS *Queen Mary* sailed from Gourock, Scotland, her passenger list included 5,000 well-guarded German prisoners of war captured by British forces and destined for detention camps in the United States. Also aboard was Prime Minister Winston Churchill and his entourage of aides and advisors, including Air Vice-Marshal George Forrest-Wainwright and his daughter. Mary was to serve as her father's companion at various state and social functions. He had explained to the PM that her past experience in dealing with high ranking members of the military and diplomatic corps would be an asset. The prime minister enthusiastically approved her presence on the trip as he believed the president could not resist being charmed by her. Although George believed all this to be true, he didn't share the true reason for her presence with the PM.

The *Queen Mary*, also known as the Grey Ghost because of her wartime gray hull and her ability to avoid detection by German U-boats, had departed on May fifth, taken a zigzag course and arrived in New York on May eleventh. Standing at the rail, Mary and her father watched as she nosed in alongside the upturned hull of the French liner *Normandie*, which had been interned in 1939 two days after Germany invaded Poland and commandeered by the U.S. government shortly after the Japanese attack on Pearl Harbor. She was renamed the *USS Lafayette* and while being converted to a troop ship she caught fire, burned, and capsized in her slip. That had happened on February ninth of 1942, and it was still not clear if it had been caused by sabotage or accident. It was known however, that the amount of water pumped into her to fight the fire is what caused her capsizing.

"What a depressing sight," Mary said, "with those mammoth propellers up in the air. Even though not caused by direct combat it must bring the sense of wartime devastation closer for New Yorkers. London knows war at home but I don't believe America has any conception of it."

Mary, with her arm tucked in her father's, then asked, "Can you tell me anything about yesterday's conference with the PM?"

"Not very much I'm allowed to repeat, but I can say that his spirits are boosted by being at sea. He took his role as First Lord of the Admiralty very seriously and I believe it was the best time of his life."

Actually, the meeting had been to develop a strategy to convince the reluctant Americans that their effort should be defeating the Germans and that the Japanese should be dealt with after. The PM had his own specific ideas on how to use Forrest-Wainwright and his daughter to achieve this.

The scene on the dock appeared to be total turmoil.

Military police and trucks were waiting for the German POWs; immigration agents and security people were swarming aboard the Queen checking everyone's papers and looking under every bunk for stowaway spies. The Churchill party, however, was escorted off the ship before anyone else and immediately taken to a line of waiting limousines surrounded by New York City police. Mary, expecting Morris to meet her, looked at all the faces lining the dock and finally, not having found him, she allowed herself to be ushered by a gruff police sergeant to the last car in the row. With one last forlorn look she got in. Already sitting in the back seat was a familiar smiling face, but not the one she wanted to see.

"You look disappointed to see me. Well, in any case, welcome to the United States. I hope you had a pleasant voyage."

"Oh, no, I'm always pleased to see you, Mr. Sherman. I was thinking about something."

Willie was still smiling, only more so now. With an edge of formality Mary asked, "What do you find so very amusing?"

"Please, it's Willie. Or William, if you wish, and I was just wondering if you were thinking about something or about someone?"

"You seem to know quite a bit. Everyone seems to know quite a bit. The PM kept winking at me as if we shared a secret. Maybe unbeknownst to me we did."

"I really don't know."

"Well, what do you know?"

"Well, I can't reveal any state secrets, but I can tell you that Morris is in Washington until tomorrow afternoon and he asked me to meet your boat."

"At least we have the same secret. That's quite a relief. Where are we going from here?"

"The Pierre hotel, where there is a room reserved in your name, or to the embassy, where I am sure they can accommodate you."

"The hotel will be fine."

Willie, sliding open the glass partition to the front seat, told the driver, an Army corporal, "Sixty-first and Fifth." He slid the opening closed.

That evening Willie, Mary, and James Roosevelt had dinner at Sardi's, several blocks west of the Harvard Club where Willie and James were members. Mary had dressed in a fashionable navy blue skirt and matching two-button jacket, while the two men wore almost identical business suits. When word of them being there spread at the club, several fellow alumni walked over and dropped by their table to find out about the beautiful young woman dining with the president's son. James explained that Mary was an old friend from London who was visiting the United States with the prime minister. After this impressive introduction, chairs were pulled up and a table made for four now had seven people squeezed together, making it difficult for the waiters to navigate. James then started to tell a story about Joseph Kennedy dropping his pants in the oval office.

"Joe was a sometimes pal of my father and as you all know he had his heart set on being the first Irish American ambassador to the court of Saint James...."

"Jimmy, you've told me this old story and I'm sure everyone here has heard it too. I really don't want my meal ruined listening to a ridiculous tale about that horrible man."

"As you wish, Mary, but it's a very funny story and you were fond of his son Jack."

"I did my duty and was polite and actually liked him until he came back from Germany impressed with having met Hitler. That put an end to my good manners."

"Like father, like son."

"But you are quite close to his father, are you not?"

"As was my father, until this war. Now there is no room for a difference of opinion on Herr Hitler. Joe Kennedy was a great help in the last election but that was before..."

Mary, looking around the table, said, "It looks like some of your Harvard pals here agree with the Kennedys. I live in London, I have seen and experienced the results of that monster being chancellor of Germany. I agree Jimmy, no room for disagreement. Are we ever going to eat?"

"You boys should go back to the club so we can have some privacy. Tell Stuffy to put your drinks on my tab."

The head waiter, looking relieved that the crowd of men had finally dispersed, came over to admonish Jimmy in a most tongue in cheek manner.

"Mr. Sardi would like to offer you a private room if you are planning to have more guests."

"No, this will be quite adequate, and if any more of those thugs show up you can stop them at the door."

Dinner was a selection of Blue Point and Cape Cod oysters followed by a mixed grill for the men and filet mignon for Mary.

"This is truly wonderful. London, of course, no longer has such food. It's truly a different world, difficult to believe we're in the same war."

WASHINGTON, D.C.
MAY 12, 1943

The president met with Morris in his White House bedroom.

"Mo, I have two very annoying disputes which I just don't have the patience for nor the time to adjudicate. We are meeting Winston at the station in a few hours and then having a dinner reception here. I want you to quietly and quickly solve both. The far easier one is the dispute between Oppenheimer and General Groves. It appears that security and secrecy are not the first priority for Oppenheimer's people. There is an open rebellion against Grove's investigation and interrogation of everyone. Wives, children, and for all I know, their pets." Reaching down to rub his dog's ears the president said, "If anyone tried to interrogate this boy they would have to count their fingers afterwards."

"I will talk to Oppie and then Groves. I do understand the general's crucial preoccupation with security. But I also understand how these people think. They've sacrificed a lot for this project and rightfully or not resent being treated as suspects. We have a family friend, a physicist, who was quite perturbed and offended at being investigated. With her husband overseas as a flight surgeon and a young son to take care of, she turned down Oppie's invitation to the project, but she did need clearance for degaussing ships. She took it all as a personal affront."

"Just solve it."

"Might you send a secret letter to Oppenheimer praising the work being done and acknowledging the sacrifice by all involved? You could add that he may share this secret correspondence with his colleagues. This might go a long way to—"

"Draft it and I will sign it. Now for the more difficult problem. My secretary of state and my wife have very different views of —"

"Mr. President, Franklin, I would rather parachute into Berlin than be on the wrong side of your wife."

"That would never happen. Eleanor thinks you are a fine young man and is quite fond of you. She often asks Jimmy if he would bring you for dinner and she has a great fondness for that fine son of yours."

Morris realized that the only way to defeat this most manipulative man was to be one himself.

"Why don't you ask that fine son of yours. She's his mother, and if you believe the newspapers he is your closest advisor."

"I need you to do this for other reasons. It regards our situation with those poor, wretched Jews. Eleanor wants us to permit thousand of them into our country. You of all people must understand that as sympathetic and understanding as we are of their plight, the risk is too great. Imagine the number of Nazi spies masquerading as Jewish refugees, not to mention uncle Joe's communist subversives among them."

"Mr. President, I don't think—"

"The woman also wants us to bomb the rail lines taking the Jews to the camps. How can we divert precious resources and put our flight crews at risk for that? We have weapons factories, airfields, and troop concentrations to destroy. I just can't do what she asks."

"And Mr. President, I can't do what you ask."

"Morris, I am asking you as your president. I'm not—"

"I have done many tasks, some of them questioned my ethical boundaries, but to do this would be unconscionable. Not, as you may think, because I am a Jew, but because this mass killing, this mass murder, is counter to all humanity, worse than the war itself. Not to make an effort to save these people is to capitulate to the Nazis; is to abandon civilization as we know it. And to put it in your court, Mr. President, it's the most unchristian thing you can do."

The president, his face reddened with anger, turned away from Morris. "You can leave now."

That afternoon Morris telephoned James in New York to locate Mary, who was not at her hotel.

"What did you say to the boss? He has cancelled his meeting with the secretary of state and told Mother he wants to have dinner alone with Winston tonight, but

I convinced him to have after-dinner drinks with all of us."

"We had a difficult conversation. I may no longer be in his good graces."

"I wouldn't be too concerned, he told me about the draft letter you proposed. He was quite impressed with your quick thinking on that."

"Where's Mary?"

"I would imagine she's in Philadelphia just about now."

"I am really not in a state for foolery."

"It's on the way to Washington, Union Station eight thirty-five this evening. I don't understand why she's so anxious to see you, but being the gentleman I am, I didn't ask any questions and put her on the train at Grand Central. We had a wonderful dinner last night with your pal Sherman. If you read any gossip about my beautiful British girlfriend, think nothing of it. It's just gossip. My somewhat jealous wife already asked me about her and of course my father, who knows everything, admonished me before he knew the facts."

"What did you tell them?"

"That Mary was Sherman's date."

"That's the best you could do. A middle-aged confirmed bachelor."

"I didn't want to stray too far from the truth."

Morris was at Union Station at eight. From the balcony overlooking the main hall all he could see was a wavering ocean of hats. Soldiers with brown garrison caps or flat officers' hats, white caps on sailors, and a myriad of other uniform headpieces worn by our allies. The station was crowded with arriving and departing passengers jostling each other as they swarmed in opposite directions. The noise level was almost a communal yell but no words were discernible. Even focusing on a couple directly below him Morris could not understand a word of their conversation, but could still ascertain that they would miss each other very much. The great hall was not a joyous place, just a busy one.

"Looking for something, mister?"

Morris turned to face two very serious men in suits and white shirts. In build they could have been twins but their features were quite different. One had black slicked down hair and a nose that looked like it had been broken several times; the other was fair with perfect equine features. The pugilist wore a green bowtie, the other a black and yellow necktie. Both men, obviously cops of some sort, towered over Morris.

"Just watching the crowd. Why do you ask?"

"Don't get smart, fella. What are you doing here?"

Morris controlled his accelerating anger, turned away from them, and resumed watching the crowd below.

"My partner here asked you a question. It would be a wise decision to answer him. Or don't you understand English? Maybe German would be easier for you."

Morris started to reach in his jacket pocket to show these two thugs his identification papers when he felt himself being shoved against the railing with each man holding one of his arms.

"What do you think you're—"

"Taking you in for questioning. You are under suspicion."

"Suspicion? Suspicion of what?"

The blond seemed to think for a moment and then pulling Morris' arm tightly up behind his back, said, "Suspicion of plotting sabotage of Union Station. OK, let's bring him in."

"You two are making a mistake, let me show you my papers."

Looking at the military identification, the unapologetic cop handed them back, let go of Morris' arm, and started to walk away.

"Rosenfelt in the White House and now a sheeny colonel!"

Morris was ready to engage them when he spotted Mary walking to the information booth, looking very purposefully at the crowd.

Morris, moving quickly without drawing attention to himself, went down the broad staircase into the mob. He could see the clock on top of the booth but lost sight of Mary. He kept thinking, "don't move, stay in one place so I can find you."

Mary hadn't spotted Morris and wasn't even sure he would be meeting her. But she did know that Jimmy would send someone. Her plan was to walk counter-clockwise around the booth until someone found her or she gave up and took a taxi to the only place she could think of. The British embassy. After a quarter turn she saw Morris. Although it seemed impossible his head was moving in a straight line through the swirling crowd.

"Mary, don't move, let me look at you."

"Rats to that!" she said, flying into his arms. "Where have you been? I've been looking for you for at least five minutes."

"I had an encounter with a talking horse and his stablemate."

"Darling, what are you... are you drunk?"

"It's really not important. I can explain later. I hope you have something clean in that bag, we have an after-dinner invitation to the White House."

Taking Mary's suitcase, Morris led her toward the exit on the far side of the station. Walking toward the taxi cue they passed one of the cops, who was leaning on a lamppost watching the crowd. Spotting Morris he gave a halfhearted salute.

"Who is that very tall man who just saluted us? What a long face. He does look remarkably like a horse. Is he, by chance, your talking horse?"

"If you look carefully you will see his partner try-ing to read a newspaper just across the street from us. Just a couple of not very nice local cops."

Morris waved the first taxi over and gave Mary's

suitcase to the driver.

"The Hay-Adams please."

Mary looked at Morris appreciatively and held his hand for the silent taxi ride. Morris had checked in earlier, expecting to avoid any formalities, but the doorman wouldn't allow him to touch Mary's bag, instead calling a bellboy over.

"What room are we in, darling?"

Morris groped around in his jacket pocket to find his room key.

"My husband always forgets our room number. Let me help you, dear." Reaching into his pocket she pulled out the room key. "There we are," she said, handing it to the bellboy while turning to Morris. "Room four-eighty-one, do you think you can remember that?"

"I truly believe I will never forget it."

In the room, finally alone together, Mary wrapped her arms around Morris. Burying her face in his chest she started to cry. "I have missed you so very much, I just want to be close." Now sobbing, Mary cried out, "Do you really love me? I need to know if you really love me."

Morris gently took her face in his two hands, looked down at her, and smiled. "My darling, you need never worry about that, never question that I love and adore you and will for as long as I live."

Pulling away and still sobbing, she said, "If we are going to the White House I must bathe and dress."

"First, are you willing to violate several laws of the

District of Columbia and come to bed with me?"

"Do we really have time?"

"Look out the window, the White House is across the street, a two-minute walk, you can see the—"

"Pull the drapes closed. I don't want to see it and I certainly don't want those old men to see us."

It was almost 10:30 when Morris and Mary met Jimmy at the entrance to the White House. He had tracked them down and called their room several times. Apparently the president and the PM were in high spirits discussing affairs of state and other more gossipy matters. They had just returned from Shangri-La, the president's retreat near Thurmont, Maryland, about sixty miles from the White House, and against doctors' advice the president had decided on a nightcap or two.

Jimmy and his two colleagues were formally stopped at the door to the president's private living room. Tom Quinn, the oversized presidential body guard, had known Jimmy since he was a boy and enjoyed torturing him now as much as he had then.

"Where do you three think you're going?"

"Hi, Tom, is my father inside?"

"Do you have some identification, anyone could claim to be the president's son. I remember some years ago a wise guy young kid trying to get to see the boss when he was governor of New York. Looked a little like you, only younger."

"Tom, please!"

Totally ignoring the presidential son, Tom turned to Morris and said, "Mr. Gold, so nice to see you again. How is that nice boy of yours? Please give him a bear hug from me."

"I will certainly do that first thing. Let me introduce you to Miss Mary Forrest-Wainwright."

"Ah, the general's daughter. Your name is on the prime minister's list. I'm very pleased to meet you."

Mary smiled and took his beefy hand in hers. "And I, you."

Quinn let go of Mary and pointing at Jimmy said, "Now, can either of you vouch for this odd-looking fellow?"

Morris, getting into the humor of his friend's discomfort, said, "Well we did meet him at our hotel, but other than that I'm not sure."

"Morris, don't encourage him, and Mary please try not to enjoy this quite so much."

Finally, Jimmy, knowing he had to go through this exercise, meekly looked down at his shoes, stepped toward Tom, and did the one thing that was required to end the stalemate. He allowed Tom to wrap his enormous arms around him and give him an affectionate bear hug, which didn't end until Jimmy whispered "second-terry."

"That's more like it, Jimmy my boy. You three are expected, let me get you inside." Tom knocked twice on the door and heard the voice familiar to millions of Americans, "Let them in, Tom."

The president was sitting in a high-backed armchair with the famous Roosevelt grin, while the prime minister was stretched out on the adjacent sofa looking somewhat like a beached whale. Both men had their jackets off and their shirt collars open. They looked quite relaxed if not slightly inebriated.

"So my boy, it seems you remembered the secret password."

"Tom and you never seem to tire of this routine."

"It's a security matter that Tom and I take very seriously. Hello Mo, very good to see you. And this stunning young woman must be Mary, the air marshal's daughter I have heard so much about. Please excuse us for not getting up. It's been a long tiring day. I believe you know my friend the PM." Churchill, seeming to come out of deep thought, acknowledged their presence with a slight wave of his hand. That was until he saw Mary. After swinging his bulk into a sitting position he stood, albeit unsteadily at first.

"Mary W, my traveling companion. I see you have met the still unforgiven Colonel Davidson. Or is it Mr. Gold?"

"Yes I have, Prime Minister, but I suspect you already knew that."

"Indeed I did," he said, smiling at her.

Although amused by this exchange the president looked at Morris with a dramatically stern expression. "Morris, Mrs. Roosevelt would like to have a chat with you. I am quite sure she is waiting for you in her study with a secret agenda. Why don't you take your most charming friend with you and come back here after you've finished. If we haven't already retired we can talk some more. And remember, while speaking with my wife, I am the president. And Mo, unlike with Winston here, all is forgiven."

Tom Quinn, unwilling to leave the president's door, directed them to the hallway leading to Mrs. Roosevelt's private study. Not a long enough walk for conversation but long enough for Mary to briefly take Morris' hand. The door was half open and they were waved in.

"Mrs. Roosevelt, allow me to introduce Mary Wainwright. She is accompanying Prime Minister Churchill and her father, Air Vice-Marshal Forrest-Wainwright, on their visit."

"Hello my dear, I have heard quite a bit about you. Is it true that you are a driver for the British government? I think that most commendable. Is it also true that you and Morris have taken a liking to each other?" Not waiting for an answer to either question, she continued. "I must warn you that when Morris and my son James get together it can be quite raucous. I am confident that my memory of the various episodes is quite different and more accurate than theirs. I hope you can come for tea some afternoon and I will share my recollections with you."

Mary, now smiling and blushing, could hardly get a word out. It seemed as if her childhood stammering had returned with the knowledge that most of Washington seemed to know of her very personal life.

"Thank you, Mrs. Roosevelt, I would love that. But please don't worry. I think I can handle those two boys."

Mary immediately realized that she had referred to Jimmy and Morris, both considerably older and seriously involved in the war effort, as "boys." She looked down and said nothing else.

"Now, as for you Morris, the president told me how you stood up to him. I believe he used the word 'defied.' Aside from being furious about not getting his way, he was delighted with your courage. He knows what a bully he can be and he is after all the president of the United States. I have suggested that he apologize to you but I don't expect that to happen. Also I must tell you how pleased I was to hear of you making a stand. Mary my dear, I'm afraid that we can't explain to you what this is all about, but in time, you will know, and be quite proud of your young man. It seems my husband chose to send you along with Morris for nefarious reasons, and please accept that I have very much enjoyed meeting you, but that man has effectively prevented any conversation of sensitive issues. He knows we would never violate the bounds of secrecy, even in front of someone as trustworthy as I am sure you are. You are after all, a foreign national traveling under the diplomatic umbrella, who might have to choose loyalties. I hope you understand."

"Of course, Mrs. Roosevelt. If I only knew where to go I would leave the two of you alone, but the White House is unfamiliar to me."

"Well I certainly hope it will become more familiar to you and that we will see more of you. For the present you should return to the president's office and try to get those two old men to go to sleep. Good night now." Picking up her telephone receiver she waved them out of her study and returned to work.

"She is as much a force as he is," Mary whispered quietly as they walked back to the president's living room.

"No, Mary, in many ways she is more of a force," he whispered back. "I can and will tell you my stories."

When they reached the door Tom Quinn was no longer there but there was a note from Jimmy resting on Tom's chair. "The world leaders have gone to bed. See you in the morning, JR."

The White House gatekeeper, who remembered Morris from past visits, called a taxi to take them to the Hay-Adams. The driver, a skinny middle-aged guy with bad teeth and a little Confederate flag on the dashboard, asked what they were doing at the White House. Not wanting to start a political discussion with a man, who just by the look of him, Morris was sure, would be vehemently against the president, said, "Just visiting an old friend who has worked there a long time."

"Well, if you ever bump into President Roosevelt or

Mrs. Roosevelt, could you tell them that Joseph Macon from Kent County, Maryland, voted for the president every time and to keep up the good work. We have a photograph of them in our bedroom, and tell Mrs. Roosevelt that it was mighty brave of her to go flying with those nigger boy pilots in Alabama. Anything for the war effort, I suppose. My wife thinks she was crazy to do it but I think crazy or not it was mighty brave of her."

Mary understood that Morris' squeeze of her hand was a warning not to say anything.

"Well, Mr. Macon, if I do bump into them I will certainly tell them of your support."

Arriving at the Hay-Adams, Colonel and Mrs. Davidson were informed of a room change. Apparently someone of influence had requested a suite for them, and their belongings had been moved to their new quarters. Morris politely but firmly insisted on being moved back to their original room or a similar one on the same floor.

"If they really want to hear what we have to say to each other they'll have to try harder than that," Morris whispered to Mary.

"It reminds me of London," Mary said, smiling. "Quite exciting all this spying on us. I do wonder who it is."

"It really doesn't matter who: Americans, British, Germans, or even Russians, there is no way of telling. It could be any one of them. But at least we are aware of it and can thwart their efforts."

"Or at least try to. I really don't know why we are so important to them, it certainly isn't me they're interested in."

"I think your evening activities would be of great interest to them."

"If you have any hope of sharing in those activities you will stop teasing me," Mary shot back.

The next morning Morris, Willie Sherman, and George Forrest-Wainwright met in another basement room, this one at a U.S. Navy medical office building on E Street. The "gang of three" had a lengthy and highly clandestine agenda. They were plotting to slow the German super-bomb development while keeping their methods a secret from their two heads of state, meeting just a mile away at the White House.

Willie was doing his now familiar pacing around the room, always avoiding the mismatched collection of chairs obviously left from a redecorating project. The table they were sitting around was white metal, with black showing through where it was chipped. A remnant of some medical office, it had unused brackets for attachments of some kind and a drain hole in the middle.

Morris spoke first. "Yesterday morning a young Russian girl approached me during my walk on the mall. It seems my movements are very well known to our allies from the east. In any event she had a message that Tommy is now in Washington and wants to meet. To be precise, the message was, 'Time is running out. We must meet very soon or not at all.' I think our friends are getting impatient for an answer and I think we should give them one."

After discussing the general parameters of a plan of how to meet Tommy in a place of their choosing, it was decided to leave the building and discuss the more troublesome aspects of their greater plan while walking outside, away from the possible presence of eavesdroppers. After going to the back courtyard, well away from the building itself, Willie opened the discussion.

"Do we all agree that our decision is warranted, that what we are doing is the right thing? That lying to our duly elected heads of state is justified? I really don't care about the ethics of it or the personal risks we're taking, but we have to be very careful. If we're wrong, the consequences will be dire."

"No more dire than if we are right and do nothing." Morris added, "This bomb, if it truly can be developed, could devastate London or New York and give Germany absolute supremacy over a formerly civilized world. I really don't see that we have any choice. Although we don't trust the Russians any more than Roosevelt or Churchill do, I believe we understand them better. We are, after all, not politicians and do not dread the public's ire or defeat at the polls. All we have to do is accept the strong possibility of a long prison sentence or the gallows."

"My oath is to king and country, not prime minister and country, so my decision is clear. I believe you two fellows have pledged to follow the instructions of your president, which is not quite the same thing."

"George, you can express it however you wish, but the fact is that this is treason for all of us."

"I truly believe there is a difference. You two will face a firing squad and I will face a hangman, but I really don't think it will come to that. This Tommy of yours will probably have already poisoned the three of us with his vodka."

"So we are absolutely clear," Morris interrupted. "Let me, once again, dissect the parameters of this scheme and confirm that we are all in full agreement." Morris presented, analyzed, and defended against the negatives of each step as if he were pleading before the Supreme Court. When he was finished, all three men were in agreement. Earlier, while still in the basement, it had been decided, for the benefit of anyone eavesdropping, that they would offer to meet Tommy at the old Cosmos Club, where Willie was a member.

This choice, which they knew would be unacceptable to Tommy because of the possibility of listeners, had a double purpose. The first being to accommodate Tommy's understandable distrust of them and his need to show his bosses in Moscow that he was in control. The second, that it gave their own suspected listeners, as Willie would put it, disinformation to get them off their trail. The real meeting, after their fictitious submission to Tommy's demands, was to be at a bench in Lafayette Park. To avoid the suspicious appearance of three men standing around, Morris and Tommy would be playing chess on a set they would bring, and Willie would be watching them play. George would be across the path keeping a watch for followers from any country. If he spotted anything worrisome he would put down his newspaper and the chess players would move on.

"Gentlemen," Morris said, "I think it's time for me to take a walk in the park and wait for my little Russian girl to find me."

After walking up and down the paths several times, Morris was finally approached by the Russian, who handed him a slip of paper and stated in a seemingly rehearsed statement, "You will arrive at the address written tomorrow morning at exactly nine-twenty. You are to be accompanied by your colleague Mr. Sherman and no other persons. There will be an automobile waiting for you."

Morris handed the address back and said, "That will not be possible. We will meet at the Cosmos Club and discuss our business there. If you will excuse me, I will now continue my walk. "

The young woman crushed the paper in her fist and quickly walked in the direction of the White House, visible through the trees. Morris watched her scattering the ever-present pigeons as she went, and then stopping to speak to a heavyset woman standing at the edge of the park. The girl then continued on toward the streetcar stop just in front of the White House.

Walking away, Morris continued to watch the other woman as she took a path that would intersect with his if they both timed it right. As they came together Morris beckoned for her to walk with him, She spoke first in a moderately heavy Russian accent.

"You refused to meet us."

"Not exactly. We very much want to meet, just not at some place unknown to us."

"As this club of yours is to us. We cannot agree to meet there."

"Let's be spontaneous."

The woman looked at him with a questioning expression. Clearly she did not understand the word.

"Let us pick a random place that will be acceptable to both parties."

"I think you already have such a place in mind. Yes?" she said with suspicion.

"No. I just now, just this moment, had an idea. Why not this very spot? Right by that bench," Morris said, pointing to his left.

"No. We will decide which bench. When we arrive here tomorrow morning at nine-twenty exactly you will discover which of the many it will be," she said with a sweeping motion of her arm to indicate all the benches on the path.

Morris silently looked down the path as if to consider her demand, and finally said, "Very well, you will decide, we accept your terms."

The meeting went almost as planned. When Morris and Willie arrived, followed at a distance by George, they spotted the heavyset Russian woman standing by a bench at the far end of the path, but no Tommy. She actually tried to smile when they reached her.

"Are we to wait for Tommy?" Morris asked.

"Today I am Tommy, tomorrow or next week some other comrade may be Tommy. But you can call me Tommy."

While walking, Willie had spotted six men lurking in the park. Three were unmistakably Russians with their oversized jackets and workers' caps. They were obviously meant to be seen. The other three looked military and could have been British, American, or even German, but definitely did not look Russian. A seventh man was sitting on a bench across the path about fifty feet away. This was George, who was reading the newspaper. As long as no one approached close enough to hear the conversation he was to continue reading, but if that changed he would put down the paper. He also was wearing a shoulder holster with Morris' .45 and was fully prepared to use it should any trouble, especially an abduction attempt, be made.

"Well then, Tommy, we are prepared to seriously consider many of your deman... rather, requests, for our cooperation, but as you can certainly understand we will need some authentication of your man. Some proof that he is who you say he is and that he has access for our benefit. Provide us with that and we will proceed."

Morris was deliberately not being specific. He knew nothing of this Tommy and could not confirm that she actually represented the Russian government. It would be up to her to reveal what she knew of the earlier Tommy's request and to establish her credentials as an authorized negotiator. Was she the real thing?

"We of course anticipated such mistrust. Proof will be delivered to you at your home in New York, where your lovely son lives with his grandmother. We had a luncheon with young David and my daughter Alina when he visited our embassy. A fine boy. I am told that he enjoys baseball in your Central Park. You must be quite fond of him."

Morris reddened with anger, but it was Willie who reacted. Quickly standing up he put his hand firmly on Tommy's shoulder and squeezing quite hard, said, "If you ever threaten this man's family again I will bring it to the attention of the president of the United States and he will personally mention it to Premier Stalin. I'm sure you are expendable."

Seeing what was happening, one of the Russian watchers started to move toward the bench, but George called out to him and lifted his newspaper, revealing his .45 aimed directly at Tommy.

Everything stopped for a tense moment and then Morris rose to his feet, glared at the Russian woman, and walked away.

The next day Morris and Mary stopped at the front desk before leaving for New York.

"Your bill has already been paid and, if you can wait one moment, we have an envelope for you."

The desk clerk went to the manager's desk and retrieved a white envelope, which Morris immediately saw had the words "The White House" engraved on its top left corner. Opening it he quickly read the short note and slipped it in his pocket without saying anything to Mary.

During the long train ride to New York they discussed many things, but the most important, to both of them, was Mary meeting David for the first time. Morris reassured her repeatedly that David would be all for her and that his grandmother would be ecstatic for both Morris and David that there was a young woman in their lives.

"This is one time I can assure you that what I predict will be what will happen. After all, he's my son, how could he not love you? And as for Sarah, you have no idea what a Jewish grandmother is. How could you? To them, their first grandson could be the messiah. She will do anything for his happiness."

"I do trust your intentions about all things, but your assuredness makes me a bit uncomfortable. Sometimes wishes overpower judgment."

"You'll see, so please stop worrying."

"Can you tell me about that mysterious letter? I couldn't miss how deferentially the clerk handled it or that it was marked White House." Morris handed her the note.

"Your stay has been paid for by your fellow American taxpayers, specifically by my father's discretionary fund. I hope you enjoyed the suite we arranged for you. Best regards, JR."

"Does this mean that—"

"It means we are not as important as we thought and that we gave up a wonderful suite for no reason. Jimmy may never let us forget this."

"But he will forgive us. It's just too ridiculous for him not to."

"And," Morris added, "he will share it with his father, who will tell and retell the story, adding his own details at will."

"Well, in a way I'm glad we only had a single room. That way you were never out of my sight."

"I did notice that you kept your eyes open."

"Really Morris, that's enough."

NEW YORK CITY
MAY 15, 1943

When they arrived in New York, David and Sarah were waiting at the station, Sarah having been forewarned by a telephone call from Morris the night before. David, clearly resisting the temptation to run down the platform, walked toward them in a slow and deliberate manner.

"Hello, Dad," he said, barely looking at his father. "And you must be Miss Wainwright," he continued, sticking his hand out with a serious look on his face. "I'm David Gold."

"Very pleased to meet you, David Gold," Mary said, taking his hand, "and please call me Mary." The question of what David should call Mary had been discussed on the train. Morris had decided that a more informal introduction would make David more comfortable and bring Mary into the circle of David, Sarah, Morris, and now Mary.

David grinned, and pointing behind him, said, "That's my Grandma standing up at the gate. She doesn't like to break the rules and the sign says Passengers Only, but I decided you needed a proper welcome. After all, you're a very long way from home and some rules are not so strict. Can she call you Mary also?"

"If she wishes to. Why don't you introduce us and let's find out." Morris was beaming as he watched David walking Mary up the ramp carrying her small satchel. His son was flirting with Mary, it could not be better.

As was predictable, Sarah took charge. It was easy for her to accept Mary. She could see that Morris was in love and that David was quite taken by her, and she too felt a bond with her. Their relationship, for Mary who had lost her mother and for Sarah who had lost her daughter, quickly took on a special closeness. They spent hours endlessly talking, and even sharing the most personal feelings. Sarah told Mary of her daughter's tragic accident and how she had tried to give David as much mothering as he would tolerate. Sometimes she knew it was too much, but her life's role had become taking care of her grandson, filling the void left by his mother's passing as much as she could. She explained that she understood that being a grandparent could never truly replace being a parent and how, maybe selfishly, she missed being less strict and more indulgent, just a grandmother. Not that Morris was not a wonderful father, but his new work with the government, with the president, kept him away much of the time.

Sarah was soon convinced that Mary was Morris' and David's gift from God. She embraced a willing Mary as her surrogate daughter and very much wanted her to meet her closest friends, especially Ivy Litvinov and Susan Marx, both of whom she had extravagantly called long distance to tell them about Mary. Morris, oblivious to most of these happenings did, however, draw the line at Sarah having a luncheon with all her friends to introduce Mary.

David, on the other hand, wanted Mary all to himself and took long excursions with her to show her New York. She hired two particularly calm horses at the Claremont Stables on Eighty-ninth Street and together they rode the bridle paths of Central Park. David had never ridden before but, although he was nervous, he didn't want to disappoint Mary, who had grown up riding. He was quick to learn and with Mary's guidance was able to confidently trot on their first outing. Not only did he come to enjoy the riding, and Mary's attention, but she had introduced him to something none of his friends had ever done.

One early morning, riding in the mist across from the pond in the park, David stopped his horse and blurted out his question.

"Do you love my dad, will you marry him?"

Mary reined in her horse and turned and smiled at David. "I think that's an answer I must save for your father."

David persisted. "Don't you think I have a right to know. He's my father and that would make you my stepmother."

"I do think you have that right, but not before your father. Let's ride." She nudged her horse and trotted off with David following.

The next morning a letter arrived containing four tickets to the new hit musical *Oklahoma*. The attached note merely read, "Compliments of Tommy."

Morris' first inclination was to tear up the tickets. He did not want his loved ones involved with unpredictable Russian agents. Tommy had been warned about involving his family, and now this, another attempt at being in charge. Or maybe just a peace gesture, an apology of sorts for the crudeness of their meeting in Washington. On further thought he decided there was no harm, at worst it was just a foolish game of power, a chess move to distract but without consequence. Why not play along with it? He was sure his family would love to go and it was the hottest show in town. As it turned out, the show was enjoyed by all. David came out humming the music, Mary wondered if the West was anything like this and Sarah believed this to be the first great American opera. Morris had received his package early on. As he sat down in an aisle seat the usher bent down and handed Morris a small brown envelope.

"I believe you dropped this."

Morris, expecting to be approached, had thanked him and slipped it in his jacket pocket.

Before dropping Mary at her hotel and continuing home they all walked over to the Russian Tea Room. There David instructed Mary on the proper way to eat Chicken Kiev without getting splattered with hot butter and she showed him what, she thought, was the best way to enjoy caviar. Right from a mother-of-pearl spoon. Everyone had a fine time, with the adults, especially Sarah who uncharacteristically got the giggles, having a little too much iced vodka. When the contagion of her laughter spread to Mary and Morris, David buried his head in his hands, utterly embarrassed by it all. After paying the bill Morris pulled Mary along with him into the middle of Fifty-seventh Street to hail a taxi and kept saying something to her, which David and Sarah, waiting on the sidewalk, couldn't hear over the blare of cars honking at the two of them.

When they finally staggered into their apartment Morris took the unopened envelope and locked it in his desk drawer, not wanting to risk any mishaps in his current state.

Early the next morning Morris pocketed the envelope and arranged to meet Willie Sherman for lunch at Mary's hotel. He called the Pierre, arranged a lunch reservation at a corner table, and placed a breakfast order to be delivered to Mary's room at 8:30. Then, after checking on David, who was fast asleep in his room, he took a taxi across town to the hotel. Walking through the ornate lobby of the Pierre, Morris half expected to be stopped and questioned, but he was allowed to get right on an elevator and taken to the fifth floor, where he quickly found Mary's room. When she finally answered his gentle tapping on the door, it became clear that he had awakened her, and that the love of his life had a hangover. Standing there carelessly wrapped in a bedsheet, trying to focus through bleary eyes and running her hands through her mussed hair, she was the most beautiful woman he had ever seen. She fell into his arms moaning, "What have you done to me? I should have stopped drinking when you and Sarah started calling it 'wadka.' Poor David. He must have been mortified by our behavior. Do you even remember what you said to me?"

"I remember every word and you must have agreed because we are no longer disrupting traffic."

"I would have agreed to anything just to get you safely off the roadway and onto the pavement."

"But you did agree to—"

"I need a cup of coffee before we have this conversation. Come to bed with me."

Looking at his watch, Morris said, "My darling, I'm afraid it's too late for that. Coffee will be here in three minutes."

"It's never too late. You go in the loo and get your clothes off. I shall open the door when the coffee arrives."

"Not dressed in that sheet you won't. I'll get the door."

After what Mary described as "lovely lovemaking" they sat in bed having coffee and cold toast, not touching the no longer appetizing cold eggs but devouring the bacon.

"You know it's not the sex, it's that I'm just so in

love with what's in here," Morris said, kissing Mary's forehead.

"Well, I'm really very sorry to hear that, as for me it's the sex. You are a nice enough bloke, and I do like how you look, but..." She then pushed him back on the bed, straddled him, held his arms down, and looking into his eyes she whispered, "Now let's have that conversation."

"I believe I'm at a disadvantage here."

"As it will always be," replied Mary.

"Is that a yes?"

"Of course it is, you ridiculous old man, but if you ever play in traffic again I will strangle you."

"I do know that I will love you forever."

"I know you truly believe that, my darling."

As Morris watched Mary getting dressed he tried to understand what she had said. It seemed as if Mary felt she could never believe in forever. Maybe there was some untold piece of her history that prevented that. Rationally, of course, she was right, but for him the exquisite feelings of absolute love overcame the rational. It didn't mean she loved him any less. It simply meant that, for her, the future literally could not be relied upon; although often exciting and exhilarating it was always unpredictable and sometimes dangerous. Mary was not a woman of blind faith. She had considered life with a rational focus he had not used. Of course she was right. He could not promise forever;

he realized that he had always known in his heart that it was unknowable, that it was actually a lie. A lie he wanted to believe, but a lie nonetheless. Still watching Mary he thought, "My darling, you are right, of course I believe I will love you forever."

Mary, as planned, left the hotel to meet David and Sarah at the Museum of Modern Art on Fifty-third Street. Susan and Harpo had recommended the exhibit, which was the sketchbooks of Diego Rivera from his time in the Soviet Union. Sarah decided that David, who was taking a few days off from school since his Dad was home, would particularly be interested in it after his visit to the Soviet embassy.

Morris, now dressed and alone, went to the closet and removed the small brown envelope from the inside pocket of his suit jacket. Sitting at the desk and slowly turning it over and over, he carefully examined it. It had two lines of elaborate cursive written on the front: "Mr. Morris Gold F101" and appeared to have no other marking. As he opened it he saw that it had been sealed with a thick dark brown glue making it impossible to open and seal again without detection. Inside he found a collection of fourteen small photographic negatives in separate glassine envelopes. Knowing he could discern very little without enlargement he wrapped everything, including the brown envelope, in Hotel Pierre stationery and slipped it in a new envelope.

Staring at it on the desk he wondered if the contents would be proof enough or just another feint in the chess game the Russians could not seem to resist playing. After one last look at Mary's room and the mussed bed Morris headed downstairs to meet Willie and turn over the negatives. Willie would pass them on to the experts at the top secret facility in Oak Ridge, Tennessee, and get a scientific opinion in the next few days. Then the "gang of three" would examine them for any other evidence and make a decision to proceed or not.

The report from Oak Ridge took longer, and was not as helpful, as expected. It was almost two weeks before a frustratingly inconclusive opinion was received. Some of the scientists believed Germany was on the correct path while others were convinced that the German progress, though scientifically impressive, would not result in a viable weapon. By this time Willie was back in Washington, David was back in school, and Mary had travelled to Canada with her father, who was reviewing RCAF training procedures. Morris, still in New York, was spending as much time as he could with David. Clearly his involvement in the war effort was going to keep him away from home for long periods, consequently any time they could spend together now felt like a gift.

Morris, Willie, and George all agreed to meet in London and finalize, as much as possible, their overall plan for disruption of Germany's progress and more specifically prepare to negotiate Russian access to the

American and British atomic research facilities. London was chosen for these meetings as they believed their basement room in the embassy to be secure and the two Americans wanted a diminished ability to brief the president on their potentially catastrophic and treasonous plans.

The three men flew to England on separate planes, Willie and Morris as passengers on bomber deliveries from upstate New York, and George, with many stops, as navigator on an RCAF de Havilland Mosquito, one of the world's fastest fighter planes.

LONDON
AUGUST 26, 1943

When the "gang of three" finally assembled in their
basement room it had been almost a month since the
Russians had provided their proof and more than two
months since their trip to America. The room had not
changed but for a thick layer of fibrous dust now covering everything. It seemed the embassy had taken Willie's instructions quite literally. No one was to enter
the room without his authorization. No exceptions.

By the time Morris and George arrived Willie
was already pacing the room, stirring up a cloud as
he moved around, and although he was using a loud
voice, it was as if he was speaking to himself. "This
was the difficult moment I have been anticipating.
How the hell do I make this work? We can't trust those
we must trust and we are misleading those who must
trust us, and those who don't trust us must..." George
stepped in, blocking Willie's path, and grabbed him by
the shoulders.

"Willie, stop. What are you talking about, whom
are you talking to? Have we lost you to madness?"

"Actually," Morris interrupted, "he makes perfect
sense to me, but none of it matters. We must accom-

modate the Russians as they must accommodate us. It has nothing to do with trust; trust will not be found, it does not exist."

Willie, having calmed himself, smiled at Morris and added, "But we must trust each other. That is of the utmost importance if we're going to succeed with this mammoth betrayal of our country's greatest secrets. So let's get to it, my friends."

It was quickly agreed that the evidence presented by the Russians demonstrating that they had a spy buried in the German super-weapon program was believable. The photographs had shown chalkboards and documents with calculations that the scientists, including Einstein, had found quite credible. In addition there was a very blurred but still discernible photograph of some long tubes and other equipment being examined by two scientists, one of whom appeared to be Werner Heisenberg, the Nobel laureate and leading German physicist; and the other Walther Gerlach, who, they knew from other sources, had just been appointed head of the vast Nazi super-weapon project.

Gerlach's presence with Heisenberg dated the photograph as being quite recent and added great credibility to the evidence. What was questionable, however, was the progress being made by the German scientists. If in truth the Germans' development was far behind the allies it would be a mistake to give the Russians access to the potentially successful work being done in

England and the United States. After much discussion it was agreed that it was better to give Stalin the bomb then to risk Hitler having it.

"Morris, I think it's time for us to take a walk and give Tommy a chance to find us. I'm sure he or she, whoever Tommy is today, is getting anxious. George, you should follow as usual. Oh, and Morris, don't forget your sidearm this time."

After picking up his .45 from the embassy guardroom Morris led the group out toward Oxford Street and almost immediately was approached by a young woman who, in a heavy Russian accent, asked directions to the Oxford Circus tube station and said, "That is the place."

As the two men being followed by George approached their destination they could see that the first Tommy was back. He was in the distance staggering toward them in his too long brown overcoat and workers' cap.

"Ah, my old friends have returned. We should arrange to have our other friends meet your other friends as well. That would be nice. Yes?"

"Hello, Tommy," Morris said, putting out his hand, which Tommy ignored. "We have much to discuss before we do that, but in principle I think it can be arranged."

"If you have consulted with your family in Washington we can meet at the place you already know."

"We have discussed the matt—"

"Good. The car is waiting up the road but I am sorry to say we do not have space for our friend the air marshal."

Willie looked down the road and saw George talking to two men who were obviously blocking his way. He waved and gave George a thumbs up sign to reassure him. George nodded, and when he turned to walk in the opposite direction the two men followed him.

As they approached the car Willie said, "We are both armed and will keep our weapons."

Tommy laughed. "Just like an American cowboy movie. OK partner."

Willie quickly answered with a smile, "I expect us to be partners in this movie, so let's get on with it."

The flat in Bayswater had been redecorated; in place of the upholstered settee there was now a round wooden table with four undersized chairs around it and, ominously on the floor in the corner of the room, a large vase filled with dead flowers. No vodka, no tea, no hospitality. This was to be a negotiation without pretense.

When they sat the fourth chair was taken by a small bespectacled man with pencils and a worn looking cardboard portfolio. Although he was not introduced he nodded at each of them, including Tommy, and started writing even before any words had been spoken.

"Do we have agreement?" Tommy asked, with a much diminished accent. Morris answered, as it had been agreed before leaving the embassy that Morris would do the negotiating and Willie would play the role of interrupter when needed.

"We do in principle, but of course many details need to be discussed before any action is taken."

"You may proceed."

"First we will need some proof that you actually represent the Soviet government and are authorized to negotiate for them."

"Those are separate proofs you require. You may watch me enter our embassy without papers, I will be recognized and accepted by the guards. You may also watch me luncheon with the First Secretary. That should be proof enough. As for authorization that is another problem altogether. You must understand that some decisions, some risks, can only be undertaken without authorization. Our leaders believe too much in their power to be trusted. I am sure it is the same in your countries. We must imagine to have some level of trust between us, even though we cannot trust each other."

"If you're to be without authorization and yet trusted, why are you permitting a secretary to keep a record of our meeting?'

"Ah, I must explain. He is my sister's husband, he does not speak any English but the transcript is still required. They are always interesting to read. He is a poet. I think you will understand this."

Willie turned to the notetaker and said in an even

but firm voice, "Stop writing, put your hands on your head or I will kill you." The man looked up at him, nodded, and resumed writing on his tablet.

Tommy smiled, reached across the table, and took the tablet from his brother-in-law. "Trust, my friend, we must trust each other. Let me translate for you. 'The first bloom of the flowers was past. Like soldiers of the great war each leaned on another in a fruitless effort to remain upright.'"

"OK, Tommy, I will trust. We accept that you had a man in place. Is he still there and how much access does he have?"

"Understand that I cannot reveal everything as he is in a very dangerous situation and of great value to us," Tommy continued, but now his speech had no trace of a Russian accent. In fact, to Morris' ears it had a slight New York or Brooklyn tinge to it. He had now dropped any pretense of being the Russian buffoon. "He is still in place and by being a very minor participant in the research he is often unnoticed, but be assured he has full access to even the most secret areas. He is fully trusted."

"What exactly do you require of us?" Morris asked.

Tommy took a piece of paper from his pocket and passed it to Morris, who read it and handed it to Willie.

It named fifteen scientists: six for the Manhattan laboratory in Los Alamos; two for Chicago; four for the Tube Alloys laboratory in Billingham, England, and three for the laboratory in Ottawa. All research was to be shared immediately upon development.

Willie looked up and said, "You appear to already have quite a bit of knowledge about our laboratories. Both Los Alamos and Tube Alloys are supposed to be highly secret. Now Tommy, since we're trusting each other, let me ask you this. Do you currently have spies at these facilities?"

"Maybe you could trust me to answer you, but I do not know. Some information has been kept from me, as I am sure it has been kept from you. But I think it's possible."

"We will have to study this list, but of course we also expect all information gathered by you to come to us immediately. You should also understand that any scientist placed at these laboratories must be reporting to you without the knowledge of any of the other scientists. They must also be spies. Only the men in this room and a few others will know their identity. This is of the utmost importance. Do you have such people?"

"This is a difficult question, it requires us to reveal those now trusted in your countries but with allegiance to ours. It will put them at great risk if exposed beyond our small circle of friends. We must protect our big secret forever. Even after we have been victorious. We must act as allies. Of course we are allies. It is only some of our leaders who fear each other. We have much in common. Though called otherwise, the socialist revolution brought your country out of economic depression and made it possible for you to mobilize and join us in this war. It is fascism that we despise, not each other. We are protecting our great countries from our enemies and from our leaders."

Morris and Willie, realizing that they had much in common with Tommy, both nodded in agreement.

"We will make this work for all of us. Willie, I believe we have a new compatriot."

"He might prefer to be called a comrade. Za lyoobóf."

"Yes, of course," Tommy said smiling. "To women."

When Morris and Willie left the meeting place they spotted George across the road leaning on a lamppost with a raincoat folded over his arm.

Crossing over, Willie looked up at the clear sky and then, pointing at the coat said, "That won't be necessary."

"It's not for the weather," George said, pulling the coat back just enough to expose the muzzle of his .45.

"I thought not, but all is peaceful and you can put that away. When I last saw you you were being muscled down Oxford street."

"It wasn't very difficult to get away from those two. In one entrance to Selfridges and out another. With all the bomb damage on the street it was difficult for them to catch up. A little too conspicuous to go running down the road looking for me. I hope they aren't going to be in too much trouble. They were quite respectful in their bullying. Nothing really forceful. I gather your meeting went well and that my presence was unnecessary."

"Unnecessary but not unappreciated. It was fortunate for you that we were taken to the same flat or you might have been waiting until it did rain."

"When I arrived my two friends were here as well so I knew it must be the correct place." George said this while waving down the road to the two Russians, who chose not to wave back.

"Let's walk together. Willie and I will brief you on our discussion with Tommy."

After their walk the three men separated, Willie going to the embassy, George to his home in Mayfair, and Morris to the Connaught. When he arrived, the familiar desk clerk, a man who seemed to be in his eighties, handed him a cable from Mary. ARRIVING GG STOP MISSING DAVID AND SARAH STOP YOU MORE.

GOUROCK, SCOTLAND
AUGUST 31, 1943

Morris knew that through George's connections with the Royal Navy he could obtain the Grey Ghost's arrival information. The ship's movements were a closely held secret and although he was sure Mary wanted him to know when, he was also sure she had not been allowed to include her arrival date in the cable. Intercepted or illicit reading of cables might be utilized by German U-boat command. The *Queen Mary* was a coveted target and Hitler had offered the equivalent of 250,000 dollars and the Iron Cross to any U-boat captain who sank her. She sailed alone in order to maximize her speed and thus far that speed and stealth had kept her out of harm's way, but Morris knew the risk was always great. Putting the danger Mary was facing out of his mind, he spoke to George, who already had the information of his daughter's arrival.

The port was Gourock, Scotland, which was over six hundred miles from London, but with George's help and several flights Morris was able to be there well before the scheduled time waiting for the great ship's arrival. Then she was there, almost invisible among the dozens of smaller ships in the harbor. Her gray superstructure, barely observable, blended with the thick mist and steely seas. As he continued to watch and the mist lifted, her immense hull became more and more visible. Finally he could see her quite clearly, surrounded by tenders and other small craft.

Morris saw Mary on the second tender coming to shore. He could see her on the deck surrounded by several men who appeared to be laughing while holding her steady as the tender rolled in the swells. At the dock it was clear that these cheerful companions were American army officers. They helped her over the gunwale and onto the quay, still talking and laughing while they jumped up next to her.

Morris slowly walked down the stone steps towards the raucous group, wondering if this was something he would have been happier not seeing. But then it all changed. One of the Americans, seeing him in the distance, pointed and yelled something that sounded like, "Are you the colonel?"

Mary looked up, saw him likewise, and immediately started running down the slippery dock. There was no avoiding it: she slipped and landed face first on the hard stone. Everyone ran toward her, watching as she got up and started running toward Morris again. A little slower but still determined, she fell into his arms.

"My god, are you hurt?"

"I think not, maybe just a few bruises and a little mortified. I love you, my darling, you cannot imagine how much I love you." With that said she kissed him hard on the mouth. Morris almost instantly pulled away, and reaching into his own mouth, removed a small object. Looking at it and then at her he said, "Mary, I think you've chipped a tooth. Are you in pain?"

"Not at all. Are you sure?"

Looking closely at her again, he smiled. "Oh yes, I'm quite sure."

Running her finger over her front teeth she said, "Oh yes, I can feel it now. Not really painful, just a little bit rough."

By this time the Americans had caught up and were standing alongside them with concerned faces. "Mary, are you OK, anything broken? We should have stopped you, I shouldn't have yelled."

"I'm fine. Just a little chipped tooth, nothing at all serious. Morris, these are my protectors, Captain Restin and lieutenants Winchell, Rockford, and Stein of the 347th Combat Engineers." The four men came to attention and saluted Morris who, even though he was not in uniform, awkwardly saluted back and, trying to sound military said, "At ease, gentlemen."

"And you must be the colonel. We are all quite envious of you, sir. Throughout the voyage Mary was referred to as the colonel's lady. You were all she could talk about."

"That's really not true. I did comment on the food and on those soldiers of yours whistling at me. I may also have queried our arrival time."

"Only a couple of dozen times."

"Well, not to complain, but we would have arrived sooner had we gone in a straight line. I know submarines and all that, but I was in a hurry."

All this was said with dark humor and Morris realized that the passage had been fraught with anxiety for all aboard. Hitler's reward was no secret.

After parting with her shipmates Morris walked Mary up the steps, where a car was waiting. Sitting next to her and holding her hand in the back seat he said, "You have two choices. We can take the train back to London tonight or stay in Greenock, just a few miles from here, and leave for London tomorrow."

"I really want my travels not to be prolonged. I'm for the train. My facilities on the ship were quite stellar so I am rested and ready for one last segment before getting home."

"Then the train it will be. We do have quite a few hours however, so I propose we find you a place to rest, that was a nasty fall. But I must say that little chip is quite endearing. Does it still not hurt?"

"No, it's fine, just a little rough to the tongue. I think, if you can bear it, I would rather stop at a restaurant where I can freshen up and have a look in a mirror. Then we can have a leisurely lunch and maybe a walk. I imagine I'll have sea legs for the rest of the day unless I can walk them off."

"Driver, will you find us a fine restaurant not too far from the train station in Greenock?"

"Aye aye, Pops. I know just the place."

Mary looked at Morris and unable to not smile, mouthed, "Pops?"

Mazzoleni's Café was a small Italian restaurant that reminded Morris of one of his favorite places in Greenwich Village. He told Mary of the many times he had been there with Ruth and how his parents had been friends of the owners and how as a child he had played in the streets with their two sons, who now ran the restaurant. They had taken it over when their parents retired and went back to Italy.

"I wonder how the parents are faring under Mussolini and how the boys are doing. They're all such very nice people. I haven't been back since Ruth died. Everything was just too emotional. I received a letter of condolence from Italy explaining how it was God's will and how Ruth was in a better place. I know they meant well, but it was just too alien to me."

"We have so much to talk about. Do you believe in heaven and hell? Because I really don't. As a little girl I realized it was a way to bribe and scare people into doing what others want."

"The orthodox, the most religious of Jews, do believe in both, but their hell only lasts for twelve months rather than eternity. It's not really clear to me if the souls of those in hell disintegrate or go to heaven after their sentence is up. Without one highest authority, pope or archbishop, its difficult to get a consensus. In any event I don't believe in any of it. I'm Jewish in a more historical and cultural way. I identify with other Jews much as a tribal member but not as a believer in any doctrine."

Mary reached across the table and took Morris' hand.

"Well if there was a heaven, being with you would be it for me."

"And," Morris replied, "if there was a hell, being without you would be mine."

The menu was adaptive of both rationing and location. They each had cullen skink, a smoked fish soup with potatoes and onions, which Mary recommended, and then a thick spaghetti with smoked salmon and cream sauce, which Morris thought sounded delicious. The waitress, an older Italian woman, who seemed to be the owner, was not happy with the combination but relented when she realized that Morris was an American and knew little of food. Lunch was less than remarkable. The soup was thick and gummy and the salmon was tasteless, but they both knew it was a meal to be remembered. After they had paid, the owner, who had either warmed up to them or taken pity on them for their poor choices, brought over two glasses of Averna, a digestive that almost instantly cured their feeling of impending death.

"Now we must have a walk. My sea legs are the least of it."

When they arrived at the rail station Morris, being an American army officer, was able to book a first class compartment. They were without baggage. Mary's was being sent from the ship directly to her father's house in Mayfair, so all she carried was a large shoulder bag filled with necessities and her gas mask. Morris had stuffed his necessities, including a change of undergarments, in his gas mask bag, leaving the actual mask in London.

They easily found their compartment about halfway down the first class carriage. Morris took off his jacket, placed it on the overhead rack, and put a newspaper down on the right side window seat. Then with his shoes off he sat on the left side and stretched his legs across with his feet on the paper. This way, he believed, he would be facing in the direction of travel. Watching him, Mary laughed. "Are you quite comfortable, Pops?" She sat down next to him with her legs stretched over his. "I was thinking of working the crossword in that newspaper but now I think not." Resting her head on his shoulder she said, "Now this is that heaven we were talking about."

As they both started to fall asleep partially entwined there was a sharp double knock on the compartment door and both of them quickly put their legs down and sat up.

"Tickets and documents please." The uniformed rail agent was dwarfed by a large man in civilian clothes holding a soft brimmed hat. His face was partially obscured; he was taller than the compartment doorway. After the formalities of Mary presenting her "Office of the Prime Minister" pass, and Morris the tickets and U.S. Army identification, the agent moved on and the large man ducked into the compartment and sat down across from them.

"Colonel Davidson, it seems you are being followed."

"You appear to know who I am, and judging from your manner and hat you appear to be a policeman of some sort. Are we talking of you following me or is it someone else? Who exactly are you?"

"My name doesn't matter but—"

"You are wrong, sir, your name and affiliation matter very much, so if you wish to speak to me you will identify yourself."

The man shrugged, and reaching into his inside jacket pocket, handed Morris a brown leather case. In doing so, intentionally or not, the handle of a pistol in his waistband was revealed to Morris.

"I see you are associated with military intelligence. Why are you following me, or are you following us?" Morris asked, handing back the identification.

"I have no interest in the air marshal's daughter," he said, looking at Mary for the first time, "and we are not following you. We are following the men who are following you."

"And who are these men?" Mary asked

"I am afraid this conversation must be confidential between the colonel and myself. If you could excuse us for a few moments, miss?"

"Of course. I'll just walk down to the dining car and have some tea. Morris, when you're finished here please join me."

Mary got up and grabbed Morris' gas mask bag.

Before he could say anything she reached in and pulled out his .45, pulled the slide to chamber a round, and pointed it at the man's head. "Now, who are you?"

The man looked startled but unafraid, Before asking any questions Morris reached over, removed the revolver from the man's waistband, and pointed at his chest.

"I am Peter Collins, a colleague of Bill Sherman, and I am here to protect you. Miss, will you please put the gun down before my children become fatherless?"

Mary didn't move. "I think we need a little more explanation before that happens. I don't know what this is all about but I do know you are not who you first claimed to be and that you wanted me out of the compartment, perhaps to do harm to my traveling companion."

"I truly am here to protect you. Mr. Sherman said you might be difficult so I thought the British military intelligence disguise would be a good introduction. If I may ask, how did you know?"

"Anyone in MI5 or MI6 who knew who my father was would refer to me as Lady Mary Forrest-Wainwright, not miss. It is not a title I earned or enjoy but I was born with it and out of respect for my father anyone in government service who knew who I am would know that. Furthermore, since I am officially part of the PM's inner circle I believe my secrecy allowance may be somewhat higher than yours."

Morris took over the questioning. "If you do work

for Sherman you will know his mannerisms."

"I don't follow you."

"Something he does that is unique to him."

"Oh, you mean the dance. It drives us crazy his gliding around the room as if on skates. Is that what you're asking about?"

"No, but it will do." Morris nodded to Mary and they both put their guns down."

"You can keep the gun, I brought it for you anyway and I have another strapped to my ankle."

Mary, not knowing Willie Sherman quite that well, didn't look convinced, and sitting down opposite Peter Collins she kept the .45 on her lap.

"It appears that two separate groups of Russians are following you. We have identified one as GRU, the Soviet Foreign Intelligence service, but the other appears to be connected with a faction of the Soviet diplomatic service led by Maxim Litvinov, the former soviet ambassador to Washington. All we can tell is that there are two separate operations seemingly unaware of each other. The GRU group seems almost amateurish compared to the others, who seem to be able to predict your movements.

"Regretfully we are not in a position to keep an effective watch over you, but we also don't see you in any immediate danger as both groups have already had plenty of opportunities to grab you or kill you."

"I believe I understand the situation and I thank

you for informing me. Please express my appreciation to Mr. Sherman."

"Lady Mary Forrest-Wainwright, please accept my apologies to you and your father. Where I come from we don't have dukes and ladies. Just plain folk."

"It's quite alright, and I hope your next masquerade is more effective."

After Willie's agent departed and they both settled themselves, Morris reached over and took the .45 from Mary and handed her the other gun. "This I believe is smaller and lighter and easier for you to hide. Willie may have had you in mind when he sent it."

"I think it's time I knew what was going on, my love. My father has told me very little. Only that he is quite fond of you and trusts you."

"I take that as a great compliment. Now, my lady. Let me jus—"

"If you continue on that path you will, I promise, regret it."

"Aw gee, I'm just plain folk. We don't know—"

"You have been warned, old man, or should I continue calling you Pops?"

On the long train ride Morris explained what was happening, going into great detail, including his meetings with Einstein and the president, and even his and Willie's last visit with Rudolph Hess. He left nothing out intentionally.

"I don't think your father will be very happy with

your new knowledge. It puts you at risk in many ways, not the least of which is a charge of espionage. I'm troubled that you are now in so deep, but I am relieved not to be keeping secrets from you."

"It will take me some time to absorb everything but, my darling, it is as it should be. We're in it together. Not that I'm afraid, but why are you so unconcerned about the Russian spies following us?"

"Quite simply, those working for Maxim are not following us, they're protecting us. There are elements in the Soviet government who want nothing to do with the West, who believe we will be mortal enemies after Germany and Japan are defeated and want any collaboration stopped. But be assured we are being well watched over."

"I think Churchill believes this too, which is why you must keep so much from him or MI5 would be charged with stopping the deal. My poor father is in such a difficult position."

"Your poor father is one of the bravest men I know."

"He really is quite brave, isn't he?"

They were stretched out as before, Mary's legs over his and her head on his shoulder. When the rocking motion of the carriage and the ticking of the rails was starting to lull them to sleep, Mary got up, pulled down the shade on the compartment door, took Morris' jacket down from overhead, and spread it over their laps. After a few moments Mary reached under the jacket and started touching Morris. "Let me do this, my sweet man."

Morris opened his drowsy eyes and whispered, "Only if you really want to."

"Yes I really want to. The feeling of you getting bigger and harder in my hand is so exciting for me but also curious at the same time. I can't imagine how it must feel. A part of your body growing bigger and bigger. I want you to tell me what it's like, what it feels like. I can't imagine." She slowly unbuttoned his trousers and reached inside to feel the skin on his stomach, then further down she took his penis in her hand, felt the heat coming from it, and gave a gentle squeeze. Morris moaned softly and turned his head to see Mary's face. "Yes my darling, let me look at you as I make this happen." Freeing him from the opening in his trousers Mary moved her hand up and down with a slowly increasing rhythm until Morris, forcing his eyes to stay open, had his orgasm while looking into Mary's eyes. Mary wiped her hand and his exhausted penis with her handkerchief. "You made quite a puddle here, sir."

"I believe you are responsible for that."

Morris reached over, kissed Mary, and started to unbutton her blouse.

"Not a chance," she said, gently moving his hand away. "You have to recover before we get to London. Then I want us to do everything. Not much chance of that now."

"I might surprise you."

"No matter, you'll just have to wait, Something for us to think about until we get there. Tell me how it feels. I mean when you get bigger and bigger and what does the climax feel like? I want to know if it feels the same as mine. What do you feel, what are you thinking when it happens, or is your mind taken over by it? It's really very exciting, we are so very different. I mean men and women, not just us in particular. Can you talk about it, I mean describe it?"

"Not easily. The French describe it as 'la petite mort.' I understand what they are getting at but it doesn't seem right to me. Let me think about it."

"If the French are right, how many do you get? Little deaths, I mean. I would hate to think they can add up to a big death. That would certainly affect our future. Of course if you need more experience before you give me any answers, it might be worth the risk."

"We can risk it."

Mary put her head on Morris's shoulder. "While you think about it maybe I can sleep until London."

LONDON
SEPTEMBER 1, 1943

When the train pulled into King's Cross station Morris saw two familiar men waiting on the platform, the same men who had blocked George on Oxford Street and then tried unsuccessfully to follow him. Since they worked for Tommy, who apparently was part of Maxim's group, they were to be appreciated rather than feared. Morris raised his hand in acknowledgment but the two men either didn't notice or ignored him.

"Colonel Davidson, welcome back. Your luggage has been delivered to your room." The desk clerk handed Morris a few envelopes and totally ignoring Mary handed him his room key. It was not a snub of Mary but discretion, something the hotel was known for. That the clerk was aware of Mary's presence was quite clear as it was her luggage that had been delivered and one of the letters was addressed to Lady Mary Forrest-Wainwright, Hotel Connaught, London, England.

"Who could be writing to you here?" he asked while handing it to her. Waiting for the lift Morris turned to see Mary reading her letter with a wry smile. In response to his questioning look she said, "It's from David. It appears that your son has done some research at the library and found my family in Burke's Peerage.

You really must read this part," she said, pointing to the second paragraph.

"When you and my dad decide to get married, does he become Lord Morris and do I get a special title? Grandma couldn't answer and I couldn't understand all the rules."

Taking the letter back Mary said, "The rest of it is quite personal."

"Should I be jealous?"

"No. You should just be happy. My father's man must have delivered my cases. One must wonder what my father is thinking, I can't imagine why he would want me out of the house. I'll have to discuss this with him."

"I think he would do anything for your happiness and sending your clothing here...."

"Let's not get carried away. These are my American clothes. Most of my things are still in the Mayfair house and the country."

"Well, my lady, the American clothes will just have to suffice for now."

"I warned you about that. Now you'll pay the price."

"And what might that be?"

"I'll think about it while soaking in a hot bath."

When Mary finished her bath she found Morris fully asleep on a side chair with his opened mail spread on his lap.

Tying her robe, she smiled. "Come on old man,

let's get you on the bed."

"I wasn't really asleep. Just resting for a moment."

"Of course you were, but why don't you just rest on the bed instead of the chair?"

Morris got up with Mary's help and staggered toward the bed.

"Maybe just for a few minutes."

After he had collapsed on the bed she loosened his necktie and pulled off his shoes. Standing back and looking down at him from the foot of the bed she knew that she wanted this to be the rest of her life. Curling up next to him, Mary put her arm around his chest, and with tears forming whispered, "I am truly in love with you, old man. I want this forever."

The next morning Mary, now in uniform, went to get a car. During the night she had decided that the best way to stay close to Morris was to be his driver once again.

"What do we have today, driver?"

"The best in the motor pool, a 1938 Riley Continental. Fast enough, naught to fifty in under fifteen. Where am I taking you, Colonel?"

"I'm not riding in the back seat." Mary was holding the back door open for him. "I'm sure you find this all very humorous, Mary, and I'm sure I deserve it after my behavior yesterday. But you know," Morris said, moving out of her striking range, "where I come from we don't have knights and lords and ladies and all that."

"We really have to stop this," she said, opening the front passenger door for him. "Where am I taking you?"

"We're picking up your father in Mayfair and then going to the embassy."

After Mary dropped Morris and her father off, she returned to the Mayfair house in order to organize her life. After a boisterous greeting from Max, her father's dog, she picked up the pile of mail and messages, mostly sent up from the country house. On top she found a calling card from Harold Dever, a former suitor known, among their friends, as Handsome Harold. She would have to disappoint the poor boy. Maybe over drinks, or maybe just introducing him to Morris would be enough. Sitting at her dressing table sorting through the mail Mary remembered that Handsome Harold was now with the Home Office. Something to do with German refugees, most of whom she assumed were Jews, but all certainly anti-Nazi. When she had last seen him he had been quite vague about his role. Not actually secretive, but ambiguous.

It had been an odd evening. Harold had acted as if he wanted to ask her or tell her something but couldn't quite bring himself up to the task and kept reverting to his charming self. He had always been fun to be with. In a group he was not unkind, but not particularly sensitive either. He had seemed a good companion but now she was no longer sure she even liked him. Maybe she never had and just played along to be sociable or to have a charming escort at parties. That he didn't seem to have much substance had never really mattered to her. Well, she didn't have time or patience for that anymore. How her life had changed. London was now going to be home. She had been living in one of their cottages at the country house and had kept a room in the city house for occasional visits, preferring to manage things from the country. Once she started driving for the army and with Morris in her life, London had become more her home. Now it was to be full time.

About a mile away Morris and George were walking the embassy grounds. Willie was not due for another hour and it was a beautiful fall morning.

"George, my friend, are you uncomfortable with my wearing an army uniform with unearned commendations?"

"I think you have earned their equal in other ways; ways that can never be recognized. But I understand your discomfort. I don't know that I deserve the medals I have been awarded. The men who served under me certainly were courageous. Following my instructions without question. Without knowing what lay ahead. Charging into the unknown with faith in their cause, that is courage. Leading others into that very same unknown is an obligation, a very different thing. I was born a man of privilege, and with privilege comes responsibility. That is obligation, not courage."

"I often wonder if putting others at risk is courage."

"Courage is... there's Willie, let's continue this later."

"Gentlemen, should we convene here? Walking seems as secure as our basement and I have progress to report. But first, Morris, did you meet my man on the train?"

"Oh yes, that was quite an adventure. You really have to train them better. Mary had him pegged in moments. George, I'm afraid your daughter is becoming involved in our adventure."

"She too has the obligations of privilege, and with you in her life it was really inevitable, but let us keep her safe."

"That's an obligation for all of us," Willie added. "Now let me bring you both up to date. As we agreed, I approached Doctor Oppenheimer and have come to an understanding with him. He will recommend new scientists to the Canadians and the British and will recruit several for Chicago and Los Alamos. Most of these men were already on his list of candidates but had been passed over for more qualified ones. None had been rejected for reasons of security."

"That says something of the ineffectiveness of your American security process and the success of Soviet infiltration. Although it helps us in this endeavor, it is worrisome."

"Morris, if you only knew the extent of useless bureaucracy trying to weed out subversives from the academic community. Not to mention the merciless politicians trying to make names for themselves attacking the innocent. It seems, however, that if we stay away from the Jews there is less scrutiny and almost anyone Oppie asks for he can have."

"I don't think that's the situation here. Although the Home Office has interned many European Jews as enemy aliens they have not interned the scientists or mathematicians because we need them. Just the working class who struggled to escape, leaving so much and so many behind. As if they could be pro-Nazi. Politicians and bureaucrats appear to be dangerous and heartlessly narcissistic bastards everywhere."

"Nothing changes," Morris added. "Read the Greeks, or Shakespeare, or the Bible. It's all the same. Willie, how much have you revealed to Oppenheimer?"

"Everything and nothing. He has been told that the leaders of the United States and Great Britain have secretly agreed to share all atomic research and that under the War Powers Act and the Official Secrets Act it would be an act of treason and a capital offense to reveal this information to anyone. I stressed that even General Groves is not cleared for this information and that Oppenheimer is among a very small group, including the prime minister and the president, who are privy to this arrangement. This I believed, correctly, would appeal to his ego."

"How did you ever convince him of this outrageously preposterous story?" George asked.

"I showed him the secret authorization document

signed by Roosevelt and Churchill. The man may be a brilliant scientist but he's no handwriting expert."

"Hah, well done my friend."

"Willie, time for a walk in the park. You and I should meet with Tommy and finalize the deal, but this time it's going to be on our turf. George can keep an eye on us as always. Let's remember that some of the Russians following us are actually protecting us from the others, who have an unknown agenda."

"You can tell the difference, the two who followed me were wearing British shoes, the others who you see around the embassy wear those heavy Russian army shoes. It's the kind of thing I notice, from many years of inspecting troops."

LONDON
SEPTEMBER 5, 1943

The next meeting was held in an elegant townhouse chosen by George. The building was surrounded by a spiked fence and had inconspicuous guards in the surrounding buildings watching the front and back. George had reached an unspoken agreement with his two Russian friends. He allowed them to follow him to the house and they didn't get so close as to be threatening or obvious. Inside, Tommy, Morris and Willie quickly reached agreement on most issues. They didn't waste time or energy on posturing. All three men knew they had the same goal: preventing the Nazis from developing their bomb. The only difficulty was when Willie explained that only twelve of Willie's people could be placed. None in Canada, where Oppenheimer didn't have enough influence, six at Los Alamos, five at Tube Alloys in England, and one in Chicago.

A compromise was reached that the other three would be cleared by Oppenheimer, given university positions, and left in place as replacements if needed. None of the fifteen would be insulated from discovery. It was their own responsibility to evade detection. If caught, the Soviets could disavow knowledge of them or not, but in no case would the Americans or British protect them in any way. If caught, they would be treated as spies.

Morris acknowledged that it had been an act of great trust for Tommy to have given him this list. He could have just turned it over to the FBI and military intelligence and been done with it. A list of scientists whose allegiances were with the Soviet Union would have been, in itself, quite a prize. They all understood that the trust of Tommy was also great, the Soviets could get the American and British atomic secrets, feed them false reports and, combined with the real secrets from Germany, build their own weapon without sharing the information. But Tommy agreed that if the Russians did not fully honor their end of the arrangement, providing information from Germany, the spies could be exposed and arrested. This, however, would only be done after an attempt had been made by Tommy to rectify the problem.

Tommy explained that there were opposing forces in Moscow who might try to scuttle their agreement and he might need some time to undo their efforts. He also vowed not to warn his people of their impending capture should that eventuality be necessary. Hopefully any disagreements could be solved before any great harm was done. Everything was based on trust between the four men.

It was a complicated and dangerous arrangement for all involved. It was not clear how much of the plan the Soviet leadership was aware of and the "gang of three" knew that Churchill and Roosevelt were not aware of it at all. They were all, it seemed, in similar danger from their respective governments.

When they were finished Tommy stood and nodded at each of them. "We are all committing treason against our governments, but treason for the right cause. We are doing the right thing."

Morris looked up at him and added, "Then again, isn't that what all spies believe?"

It was a somber parting, without handshakes or farewells. Tommy left first, followed a few moments later by Morris and Willie, who met George across the street standing about twenty yards from the two Russians who were conferring with Tommy.

"I suggest we go to my home in Mayfair, have a drink, and discuss our next steps. It's secure of any listening devices and more private than the embassy. Everyone seems to know who and where we are in any event, so why not be comfortable? We'll be alone except for my batman, Corporal Singh, and Mary. Both have been with me over thirty years and can be trusted."

The Forrest-Wainwright townhouse was an elegant white stone building, seven windows across with an arched entranceway topped by a small balcony.

"My grandfather built this house in the eighteen-twenties for his mistress. Over the years it has been used by various family members when in London, but never on a full-time basis. We have always been more of a country lot and it's only since my wife passed that it has become my principal residence. I needed a sea change and this has provided it. Mary though, seemed to prefer the country, where she can ride and be at peace and maybe be closer to her mother's memory. Now, of course, she has both boots in the war effort and spends more time here. Both of you can make this your billet if you wish. Plenty of room and I could use the company."

"A very tempting offer, George, and I do appreciate it, but I'm better off at the embassy with the code room and access to the Marine contingent and others."

"Morris?"

"It's complicated. I'm not sure..."

"Morris, do you really think I am not aware? Mary has already approved the idea and, contrary to what you might expect from this old father, I'm all for it. Please do join us."

"Let me discuss it with Mary before I answer you."

"It was her idea."

"Still, I think it best that we discuss it first."

"Gentlemen, as interesting as this conversation has become, do you think we can go inside and get on with our conspiracy? George, would you please unlock your door?"

"No need." George reached out and opened the unlocked front door. Sitting at the foot of a grand staircase about twenty feet away was a very large and very attentive German Shepherd. The moment George smiled the dog came forward, halfway, and sat in front of the three men, looking up at them. "This is Max, a gift from one of my Czechoslovakian Spitfire pilots. He brought the pregnant mother over in thirty-nine. We don't know very much about Max's father. He may be working for the Germans or, as I prefer to believe, for the Czech underground."

George raised his hand and beckoned the dog forward. Max approached, fully alert but without hesitation. Then George, in a barely audible voice, said, "Max. As you were." The dog visibly relaxed, wagged his tail, and greeted each of the newcomers with a good sniffing. "He'll quickly get to know each of you, but I advise not trying to pocket any of the silver or attempting the *Times* crossword before I do. He's a one man dog, very protective of me, and we truly do understand each other, but I'm not his favorite. As you will see, Mary is the true love of his life."

The three men, followed closely by Max, went to the library. A room infused with a decades old scent of leather, tweed, whiskey, and tobacco. A scent as powerful as a man's cologne. They poured themselves drinks from the crystal decanter, sat in overstuffed leather chairs, and released a collective sigh of comfort.

It was quickly decided that Willie should return to the embassy and make arrangements to meet Oppenheimer in the States as soon as possible, and that Morris and George would get as much believable information as they could from the Russians and use the RAF and MI6 to slow down German research. It was possible that by combining information from all their sources they could pinpoint the laboratories and factories working on the super-bomb as well as on the new jet engine aircraft, and by bomber raid and sabotage hinder progress.

After three weeks of wrangling with General Grove's autocratic minions, Oppenheimer was finally able to get his new scientists approved. Between financial, political, and security reviews and his inability to be truthful about the reason for these new recruits, his task had been time consuming. If it had not been for the secret instructions from the president and the prime minister, he would have balked at valuable time being taken away from bomb development. In England, his recommendations appeared to carry more weight than in the States and he had no difficulty placing the new personnel at Tube Alloys. He also, as predicted by Willie, quite enjoyed being privy to higher level secrets than was General Leslie Groves, his nemesis on the Manhattan Project. He assumed now that he, not the general, was truly the president's man.

Now that the Russian spy scientists were in place it was time for Tommy to reciprocate with more information from Germany. This came in the form of barely legible small negatives of chalkboard diagrams, which when analyzed were the specifications for a kind of large bore gun powered by cordite or gunpowder. Although the "gang of three" still did not know the position held by the Russian spy, it was clear that he had access to the laboratory as Oppenheimer seemed quite excited by the new documents and believed them to be authentic. The problem at Los Alamos had been developing a method of initializing the atomic reaction in a self-contained bomb. These diagrams showed a method they had not yet tried: using conventional gunpowder to create the extreme and focused force needed. It was an elegant solution, which might just work. A team including one of the newly arrived Russian spies was assigned to the task of developing such a device, but it was obvious to all involved that if this was a workable trigger, the Germans were far ahead and the Allies might not be able to catch up. The German bomb could be ready in months, not years. Some way of delaying or stopping their progress had to be found.

George and Morris, now meeting daily over breakfast, were trying to find ways of hampering the German bomb project. Attacks on the most protected sites in Germany were carried out by the RAF, losses of bomber crews were horrific, and there was no way of telling how effective the raids had been or if the sites were even actually home to jet engine research or bomb development. Because Tommy had misled them on the location of the bomb, it was a very costly, haphazard, and scattered approach, which diverted resources from other military targets and angered many in the high command who resented George's close ties with the PM. Churchill, although in the dark about the spy network and the exchange of information, was wholly supportive of the effort to stop German atomic research and bullied his commanders into following George's directives. Initially there had been concern that Tommy's spy, whose loss would be devastating, was being placed in danger by the bombings, but Tommy reassured them that the spy was quite safe as he was only on site in the evenings and that the actual laboratory was deep in a bombproof bunker.

Morris and Mary had agreed that a move to the Mayfair house would only be acceptable if they preagreed to some rules. They would not share a bed or reveal any mutual affection to the staff. It was quite important to Mary that their relationship remain private even though two of the most powerful men in the world seemed to know about it. One of them, Churchill himself, even encouraged it by inviting Mary, her father, and Morris to Chequers, the prime minister's retreat, which had recently undergone security and camouflage renovations.

In response to the invitation, Morris remarked that, "At least the Germans won't know what you and I are up to." Mary's only comment was, "We won't be up to anything. Not in that place. All those people, including the old man himself, can just put their dirty minds to rest."

"I believe you're being extremely unfair."

"You don't know my countrymen as well as I do. And the women are no better. Suppressed youth leaves too much to the imagination."

"My personal exper—"

Mary put her finger on Morris' lips and shaking her head said, "Not another word."

At one breakfast meeting George took up the disheartening truth that they had no evidence that the massive raids on Germany and occupied Europe had accomplished anything in relation to bomb development.

"Of course it has all helped the war effort and the Nazis are suffering, but if we fail, all the loss of life on both sides will have been for naught."

"We need an alternative plan. As my son has explained to me, if you are pitching, you always back up the catcher on a play at home."

"What in god's name are you trying to say?" George asked.

"It's a baseball analogy."

"As if that explains everything. How is David, he must be thirteen or fourteen by now?"

"Almost fourteen."

"Mary is really quite fond of him. I believe they correspond with each other rather frequently."

"They really became close when we were in the States. Mary knows more about David's day-to-day life than I do. Actually, your daughter is the one to ask about my baseball analogy. I'm sure she's been totally indoctrinated in the finer points of the game."

"I will certainly do that, and ask her to bore you

with the mundane rules of cricket."

"Getting back to our dilemma. I have been considering several possibilities for a backup plan, but none seems feasible."

"One, I'm sure, involves sabotage of the laboratory where Tommy's man works. I wonder if he's capable of doing something like that. The biggest negative to that action is that it would stop our flow of information, which is actually doubling our research and, in any event, I don't think the Russians would agree."

"For all your reasons and one more it is not an acceptable option."

George looked at Morris quizzically. "And that is?"

"What if our sabotage accidentally sets off the bomb? No one, including Einstein, seems to know for sure what will happen."

"If only we could steal it. Somehow get a team of commandos into the site and remove the device. Even though it appears to be impossible, we should explore the possibilities. We do know that our raids on the hydroelectric plant in Norway were successful and have probably, if we are to believe the scientists, prevented the Germans from assembling enough material to make more than one bomb."

"So if we can get our hands on this one wretched bomb our undertaking is accomplished."

"Let's continue this discussion tonight. I have a meeting—or you might say a battle to fight—with central bomber command this morning. It could be something will come to us, and perhaps you should cable Willie to get his thinking. Maybe he can find out how much the bloody thing probably weighs and how big it is. No point breaking in if we can't get it out the door."

When Morris arrived at the house that evening he walked in on Mary trying to explain the baseball analogy to her father.

"No, no. Let me take a different tack. It's the end of the final inning, that's called the bottom of the ninth, but that doesn't matter."

"If it doesn't matter, why are you telling it to me? My lord, are you trying to explain or confuse?"

"I really don't understand your difficulty with this. When David explained it to me it seemed quite straightforward."

"Enough. I understand that if you don't do what you're supposed to do the game may be lost and if you do do it correctly maybe it won't be lost."

"I guess that's the point Morris was making."

"Unfortunately, in this instance it's more than a game."

Mary put her hand on her father's cheek and said, "I know, Daddy, it's all pretty terrifying. You look so tired, are you quite alright? You and Morris will figure out a solution. I just know it."

Max, who had been listening intently to this conversation, got up and trotted to the door with tail wagging.

"Welcome home, Morris, you're rescuing me from

my daughter's inability to explain a game that your son was able to clearly explain to her. I'm quite certain you would really enjoy taking part in the discussion."

"No, I really don't think so, but I will take a drink."

"A martini?"

"If it's not the president's recipe."

Laughing, Mary said, "That truly was godawful wasn't it?"

"Actually, this comes from the PM himself and it's quite simple. You pour cold dry gin into a glass, look in the direction of France, and add an olive. If you're disoriented and can't determine where France is, you may give a glance—but only a passing glance—at the bottle of vermouth instead."

After George made the martinis he directed Mary and Morris to sit at the ivory inlaid card table in the corner of the library. This was where, as a child, Mary had been told of the death of her first dog, Ruffles, and it had become a place to be avoided ever since.

Still standing, and looking at a painting of his late wife, he said, "I have a very frightening idea." His tone made it clear that this was not being said with levity. "And I want both of you to hear me out before asking any questions. It's very important to me that you be here, Mary, as you represent the next generation and the outcome of this will be yours to live with."

Turning to face them, George continued, "I am proposing that we get the bomb from the Germans in a very dangerous way, so dangerous and so outrageous that I dare not mention it to anyone outside this room. But let me go back a bit. This morning at my meeting with bomber command we discussed the problem of dud bombs and how to reduce the number of duds we drop on every raid. It seems that a not negligible number of defective bombs are dropped by both sides. At the meeting, several ordnance experts presented the problem and explained that to keep the bomb production levels as high as possible, the fuse manufacturers have to use more readily available and less desirable materials. The result is that the number of duds is less significant than the reduction in production that would result from higher quality fuses. And, of course, we have also seen the effect of duds here in London.

"Unexploded bombs cause panic until they can be defused. The Germans have been dropping delayed fuse bombs for just that purpose. Our bomb disposal teams never know until they are in the hole if it's a time delay or a dud."

George sat down and paused as if deciding to continue or not. He started speaking again, rapidly, trying to get it all out in the open as quickly as possible.

"Now comes the difficult part. As you know, bombs are quite sturdy and, if they don't explode, they survive their fall. I'm thinking that we get our Russian friend to disarm the bomb and allow the Germans to drop it on their target so we can recover it intact. Well, that's the idea."

Morris and Mary stared at George in silence.

"Well, at least say you think I've gone mad."

Mary looked down as if examining the inlay on the table and asked, "What do you think their target would be?"

"London," was the almost simultaneous whispered reply from both men.

"George, I really don't know what to think, but I do know we all need another drink before we continue this conversation. Would you make them while I catch my breath?"

Mary spoke first. "How will this really help? Won't the Germans just make another bomb?"

"It seems," Morris answered, "that we have prevented that by destroying their supply of what is called heavy water and, by our bombing and sabotage, prevented more from being produced. The Germans are limited to one bomb. At least that's what our experts believe."

Carrying the three fresh martinis to the table George added, "It will not only stop the Germans but it will give us a working bomb to dissect. They may have the science but we will have the bomb."

"And," Mary asked, "the resources to duplicate it and build more of them?"

"The difficulty, and this is most secret information, is the fuse. We have the atomic ingredients but have not been able to invent a reliable way to explode them in a bomb. If we can capture the German fuse mechanism intact we will have it." The conversation continued through dinner. All three kept returning to the most important question. "Can we trust the Russians?" It was close to midnight before they finally said goodnight. George and Mary to their third floor bedrooms and Morris to his on the second floor.

Later that night Morris awoke to find that the house rules had changed. Pressed against his back with her arms around him was Mary. After a moment or two of clearing thoughts and vision he realized that the gentle snoring that had awakened him was not in synchronization with Mary's breathing, which he could feel against his neck, but was coming from Max, whose large body was curled up and blocking the door. Normally Max would sleep on the second floor landing within sight of George's bedroom and the front door, but tonight, it seemed, he thought he had more to protect than the family silver.

"Don't worry, he can keep a secret," she murmured. "We think his father is in the underground."

"Since he was privy to last night's conversation, I certainly hope so."

"My darling, after that conversation I really didn't want to sleep without you. We slipped in after you were asleep. I hope you're not upset."

Morris turned so he was facing her, and gently kissing her forehead said, "This is the nicest awakening I've ever had. I'm so very much in love with you.

Before falling asleep I was thinking that there is every reason to, and no reason not to, get married as soon as possible."

"The last time you asked me, if you are asking me, you were quite drunk and standing in the middle of a very busy roadway. I think I saved your life that evening by saying yes."

"Not only did you save my life but you said yes again the very next day when I was perfectly sober."

"And it's still yes and will always be yes."

"I want David and his grandmother to be there but I don't know how we can make that happen."

"Don't underestimate your son. He knows that the war makes some things more difficult. I think he will be very happy about this and I did promise him that he would be the second person to know about it."

"I presume your father is the first."

"Sometimes I wonder what attracts me to you. You can be such an idiot."

"I can't think who..."

"You, of course. You will be, no you are, the first to know."

The letter to David was sent in the diplomatic pouch and hand-delivered to the apartment in New York. In the corner below the embassy seal Mary, not wanting it to give the wrong impression, had written GOOD NEWS.

In the letter they promised to celebrate when they were all together again and asked David to share the news with his grandmother.

George seemed quite pleased by the decision. "You know your mother would have liked you to have a beautiful church wedding or...but I think for many reasons that can't be. And I believe waiting to celebrate is the right choice. Let us be together as one family and hopefully David will come to think of me as a grandfather."

Willie, back in London, tried to act as if he did not already know but couldn't resist congratulating them, and it quickly became clear that unencoded diplomatic mail was not safe from prying eyes. They received a cable from Jimmy Roosevelt. MOTHER TELLS ME CONGRATULATIONS IN ORDER STOP FATHER NOT SURPRISED JR

"You should never have used the embassy pouch to send that letter," Willie explained. "All unencoded mail is checked and censored in case the bag is captured and Morris' name is red flagged by the White House as highest priority. Someone must have copied the letter and sent it on to the boss. He loves secrets, especially happy ones."

By the end of the following week George had made most of the wedding arrangements. There would be a civil ceremony at the registry office and then a small private luncheon at the house.

But he still had one more wedding matter to take care of. This he accomplished while walking with Morris to the embassy.

"Before we meet with Willie I want to offer—no, suggest something. I would be delighted if you would give Mary her grandmother's engagement ring, that is unless you and Mary have other plans."

"Actually we already discussed rings and haven't resolved anything. My grandmother's ring went to Ruth, David's mother, and we felt it should go to him when he has a need for it. I think yours is a wonderful idea and will make Mary very happy, but as you well know she really doesn't like surprises, so I had better ask her first."

Arriving at the embassy they went directly to the basement room. The embassy had been chosen for this meeting so they would have access to the code room. A special link had been set up for transatlantic wireless communication from the embassy in London to the U.S. embassy in Ottawa. The signal was then transcribed and sent, still encoded, by cable to Washington. In this way the messages were separated from military and intelligence service communications, appeared to be routine communication from the U.S. embassy in Canada to the Office of Canadian Affairs at the state department, and would never draw enough attention to be scrutinized by government agencies or the White House. The OCA was actually a mail drop for Willie Sherman's people.

When they arrived at the basement room Willie looked exhausted. Although trying to be his upbeat, cheerful self it was clear that his trip to Washington had not gone well.

"We're going into our third year without any demonstrable progress. Maybe we have slowed the German bomb development, maybe we have credible secrets from the Russians, and maybe we have achieved nothing. The boss is tired and not looking that well and the vice president is a political hack, a haberdasher turned politician, who is unaware of any of this. He hasn't even been made aware of the Manhattan Project. I'm afraid things are on the verge of falling apart. We need to do more."

George replied first. "Morris and I have come up with a plan to get the German bomb. It involves huge risks and we both believe the president and especially the PM must be party to it."

George and Morris spent the next hour describing their scheme to a silent Willie.

When they finished, Willie whistled.

"Well, it does have one thing going for it," he said. "It has no political implications for Churchill or FDR."

"How do you see that?" Morris asked.

"Well, if it fails and London is obliterated, we will have lost the war and there will be no elections to lose, and if it succeeds no one can be told of it."

"I hope we can come up with a more reassuring way to convince the two great men."

"England is of course at the greatest risk, so I believe

Churchill needs to be convinced before the president. If he approves it will be difficult for FDR to disagree."

"We have much to do before we can approach the PM," Morris added. "We need every question answered, we need to know how to defuse the bomb with absolute certainty, and we need to negotiate with the Russians. They won't do this without some compensation."

"And," George added, "our most difficult task will be convincing the PM to trust them. That will require a true sea change in his thinking. Willie, you seem to want to add something."

"You presented this as a backup plan. Failure would be catastrophic. Let's not run with it until we truly believe our other efforts have failed. Our best solution is still stopping the German bomb. I'm afraid of this plan becoming an unstoppable freight train, the Armageddon Express."

"I agree," Morris said. "When we thought Tommy let slip that the laboratory was in Hamburg we destroyed much of the city to such a degree that we thought we had exploded the atomic device. We dropped nine thousand tons of explosives and the resulting fire storm created a fifteen-hundred-foot tornado. We accomplished nothing but the destruction of eight square miles of a populated city. God knows how many civilians died."

"We will carry the repercussions of that mistake forever, especially now that we believe Tommy misled us intentionally. The Russians want Germany destroyed, nothing but burned earth after the war. George, I haven't changed my mind, but the question I believe Willie and I still have is, after that, after Hamburg, how can we trust the Russians?"

"I understand the risks, and they are terrifying risks, but I really don't believe Uncle Joe has any interest in destroying London. Germany is a very different situation, the hatred has been earned. The greater risk for London is that the Germans develop this awful bomb before we do, not that the Russians will double-cross us."

"OK, let's slow the train down but keep it on track. I think Willie and I should have another talk with Tommy, confront him with his role in the Hamburg disaster, and try to get an understanding of Russian intentions. George, maybe you can figure out how to protect the bomb-carrying plane from our defenses. We don't want it shot down over the channel."

"I'll delve into that. On a more pleasant note, don't forget Friday at the registry. Especially you, Morris."

"Can you arrange for a few photographs that I can send home to David and his grandmother?"

"I don't think that will be a problem," George answered with a laugh.

"Getting back to our conspiracy, Morris, let me know the when and where for our meeting with Tommy. And now if you'll both excuse me, I'm off to the code room to ask Oppie how we can defuse the damn thing."

Friday was drab, the temperature just above freezing. When they arrived at the Caxton Hall registry office in Westminster there was a small crowd gathered for some other wedding. Most of the men and women were in uniform and having a grand time until George, in full regalia as air vice-marshal with the Victoria Cross on his chest, exited the car. Seeing their discomfort, he quickly returned their salute, put everyone at ease, and walked over to the wedding party. He congratulated the groom, an RAF flight officer, and the bride, a WREN petty officer. This encounter clearly was a great addition to their wedding celebration as the groom remarked, "The icing on the cake. Can't think of a better honor, thank you, sir."

The crowd came to attention and saluted George as he walked into the hall with Mary and Max at his side. Morris and Willie were already there. Aside from a slight growl at the attendant, who, after suggesting that the dog be left outside, escorted them to a small private room, all seemed to proceed as planned. As they began arranging themselves for the ceremony Max came to attention with fur raised. He growled, and barked a warning. There was a very loud knock at the door followed by the entrance of three quite burly men, whom Morris immediately recognized as police.

"I seem to have shocked a happy couple and their wedding party just outside. I assume I'm in the right place at the right time." The prime minister was framed in the doorway, wearing his typical dark suit and bowtie, and carrying that so familiar hat under his arm. When the air vice-marshal told me the good news I immediately volunteered to officiate. Having an American mother I believe exceptionally qualifies me for this task. But we must hurry, I have an appointment with the dreaded press at half past."

Max took particular notice of the newcomers and positioned himself between the prime minister and Mary, making it clear that he was not to be trifled with.

From that moment on the wedding was in the hands of the PM. He spoke briefly of his fondness for Mary and of how he had known for some time that this day would come but that he was quite unsure of this man Gold, or Davidson, whom he had planned to imprison. He then read the required text, interspersed with some momentous words of his own, elicited the I dos, and nodded that he was finished speaking. George then took a small cloth package from his pocket and put it on the floor in front of Morris. "This is from David's grandmother. I think you know what to do."

Morris, not holding back his tears, lifted his foot and stamped down on the wrapped wine glass signaling, in the Jewish tradition, the end of the wedding. They then posed for photographs with George, Willie, Max, and the PM surrounding the newlyweds.

That evening after their dinner of roast chicken with potatoes, canned beans and fresh carrots, George served a 1936 bottle of Dom Pérignon and later port with cheddar cheese. The chicken had come from the Savoy hotel, which had its own hens to supply its restaurant with eggs, and the cheese was "government cheddar," the only cheese allowed due to rationing. The dinner was a great success, with almost no mention of the war.

That night Max, seeming to understand the new status of Morris and Mary's relationship, resumed his station on the second floor landing and George, praising him for his past diligence, went to bed.

"I think David will love the photographs of the five, or rather the six, of us. Father was quite handsome in full dress, don't you think?"

"Also quite impressive. That other wedding party didn't miss the Victoria Cross. Probably off at their pub, not being believed, talking about the air vice-marshal with a VC and the PM wishing them well. "

"I think father dressed more for David's benefit than anyone else. He really isn't one to strut."

"I can't imagine your father ever strutting; even in full dress he's the most unpretentious man I know."

The next morning at the breakfast table, George spoke first. "While shaving this morning I realized that it is as if we have our own little war. We rarely discuss the greater events going on around us. We all know there is an upcoming invasion but we don't know where or when. Never have we discussed the possibilities or the strategy we think will be used. Our troops have captured Addis Ababa, the siege of Leningrad appears to be broken, and de Gaulle has taken command of all Free French forces, including the communists. Daily major events that don't seem part of our war. We repeatedly take resources from other missions. Is this right? Or are we so very self-involved? Do we really believe our mission is so crucial that it trumps all else?"

Morris took a moment before answering. "I believe it is, but I'm sure many others feel the same way about their missions. Most everyone believes that the war is ours to win. The unhindered industrial might of the U.S. and Canada seems unstoppable and the troops preparing for the invasion, the fighter and bomber squadrons, MI5 and the underground in all the occupied countries may feel that, although we will eventually win the war, without their success the war could go on for many pointless years, causing millions of unnecessary casualties. The difference is that our failure could end the war straightaway, and not in our favor."

"Of course I agree. I think sometimes I just need reassurance that our actions are justified. Here we are lying to our superiors and playing footsie with our allies of convenience, the Russians, who repeatedly lie to us."

That afternoon they met at a safe house in Bayswater. After a warm greeting in the vestibule, where Tommy wanted to embrace each of them, they went up to the parlor in the second floor flat. This was the safest room in the house, with its windows boarded up from bomb damage and old mattresses leaning against the walls to deaden any listening device. There were four wooden chairs on a round rug in the middle of the room. The house was well maintained in its dilapidated state by Mrs. Brown, who lived in number 12, next door. Both of her sons were in service and knew nothing of their mother's involvement in the war effort. She had been employed by George's family and had come out of retirement at his request. When the safe house was being used she would watch the road from her front window and was able to warn the occupants with an old-fashioned bell on a string running between the two buildings.

After the coconspirators sat, Morris explained the new plan. When he then started to question the Hamburg deceit, Tommy interrupted him with a pronouncement.

"The German bomb is going to be moved out of the laboratory and placed in a new location. If you pursue this plan of yours we have only a few weeks, a month at the most, to make the bomb inoperable. Hitler's secret weapon is almost ready for deployment."

Willie, not to be deterred, said, "I must admit my concern that this is just another red herring from your bosses. Hamburg didn't help our mutual trust. It places us in a most difficult situation. Are we to risk having catastrophic results because of your... your military's intractability? Will they listen to Litvinov or will they allow London to be destroyed? How can we trust you?"

"My friend, we are allies in this. I don't know the

saying 'red herring,' but I sense the meaning. I am as upset by the Hamburg bombings as you. I too was misled and will always feel responsible for the results of misleading you, but we must move ahead together."

"I appreciate your words, but we need more. We need more information. Who is your spy and where is he? How reliable is he? Where is the bomb laboratory? We need answers and don't have the patience for any more deceptions. If, as you say, we truly are allies, now is the time for you to prove it or—"

Morris interrupted. "Tommy, I do trust you but Willie has a point: Can we trust those around you? Who is in charge and what are their intentions?"

"I will be totally honest with you. I don't know who is in charge, Litvinov is hated by the NKVD, the army, and probably Comrade Stalin himself. He is a Jew and not to be trusted, but he does have some control, enough I think to make this plan of yours work. I hope you will trust in me because our little plot will undoubtedly earn me a bullet and I would hate to have made Sasha and Anna orphans for no reason. If it works, a bullet to keep me quiet, and if it fails, a bullet as retribution."

"Spoken as a true Russian. Tommy, your expectations are often darker than reality. You and Morris have much in common."

"Please, from now on I am Vadim. Let us be truthful about everything. We are on the same side even if we are not. Do you understand what my words are saying to you?"

"Let's begin then," Morris said, "Where is your spy and do you trust him?"

"I have come to trust her. Except for that one time, her information that could be confirmed in other ways has all proved to be correct."

"And that once was?"

"Ah, completely understandable but not acceptable. It was the location of the laboratory. She didn't want to be bombed to death. It will not happen again."

"How can you be sure of that?"

"She had two children, now only one."

Morris looked at the Russian with horror. "Are you saying that—"

Willie cut him off. "It's no more than we would have done to save thousands of lives. Is one child worth more? When we bomb cities don't thousands of children die for the greater good? Vadim, please continue."

"She's the cleaning person for the laboratory, almost unnoticeable. During her night work she has access to everything and is watched over by one guard, who she brings schnapps. He often sleeps in a chair while she does her work. I believe she now understands that she must take any risk we ask of her."

"I would expect so," Morris said. "We need her to defuse the bomb, Willie can explain."

"It's a rather simple task but time consuming. From the drawings you supplied there should be four small cloth or silk bags filled with cordite waiting for insertion or already in the bomb. Either way she needs to replace these with bags of harmless powder. If the bags are already in the bomb, as we hope, it will take about half an hour to open the access panel and replace them. If they have not yet been inserted she will have to switch them for identical bags. This is problematic as we don't really know what they look like. So our first question is have they been inserted yet? If not, we need to get photographs of the bags and use something matching their true color.

"I know this sounds simplistic, but any other method could be detected when the bomb circuits are tested, as they surely will be. We will give you a harmless faux cordite recipe."

Morris looked at Willie. "She's simply a cleaning woman. How can we expect her to accomplish this without being trained?"

Vadim interrupted. "She's a scientist, trained at the Bauman Moscow Higher Technical School, this should not be our problem. I will do this for you, my friends. I will require her to do what you need and then I will try to rescue her from the Germans and send her home."

Their next meeting was set for Monday of the following week, when hopefully they would have all the information needed.

As they waited to leave after giving Vadim a head start, Morris asked Willie, "Send her home to what? To what remains of her family, I suppose. Well, that's better than being captured by the Germans. How does he live with himself?"

"I think he is as horrified as we are by what must be done. I've come to understand him. This is a good man forced to do terrible things."

"Much like we are, I suppose," Morris said, quickly leaving the building.

LONDON

SEPTEMBER 20, 1943

The following Monday they received the information, and it was not good. The cordite was not yet loaded and was kept in a separate location unknown to the Russian cleaning woman. The German plan was to load it at the last minute. The bomb was to be moved to a secret airfield, or Fliegerhorst, in Venlo, about 350 miles from London, armed and then suspended under an Arado Jet Bomber for delivery to its target. The timeline for this maneuver was unknown.

"This isn't good news. Obviously the Nazis have their jet plane operational. There must be a way to delay things so we can come up with a new plan. We must get our hands on this device," Willie said to no one in particular.

Vadim was the first to answer. "We have devised a plan."

"Who is we?"

"Some close associates, who if revealed would be shot. I'm sure you understand. If you were to bomb the airbase it would be suspicious. But if we were to arrange a small raid on the town it would not be. The Dutch resistance could cross over and explode some rail tracks. Nothing very large or out of the ordinary but still maybe enough to delay moving the bomb."

"I think it's a fine idea but I would prefer several raids in nearby towns as well. Let the Germans believe they have a problem with the partisans. With only one bomb available to them I don't believe they'll risk a random attack."

After Vadim assured them that the Dutch communist resistance group would be instructed to execute multiple raids on the area, he left them to devise a new plan among themselves. This took almost 24 hours and many transatlantic cables routed through Canada.

The new plan, devised by the experts at Los Alamos, was far more difficult.

Willie explained, "It involves blocking the electric current to the firing mechanism, which will, hopefully, prevent the cordite from exploding. The plan has two major problems. First, it is time consuming. Even if our cleaning lady has the skill she would need at least a hour to open, rewire, and close up the bomb. But most importantly, the rewiring might be revealed when the circuits are tested. Our hope is that the short circuit is close enough to the firing mechanism that the Germans won't dare test it at the last moment and that if they do the low current of the test will not melt the soft wire she has installed. We do know that, taking into account the altitude and thus the ambient temperature when the bomb is dropped, which is a guess on our part, that the current required to set off the bomb should melt the wire before it reaches the cordite—"

Morris interrupted. "This is beginning to get too complicated for me. Will it work?"

"Maybe."

"I don't think maybe is good enough."

"Look, Morris, London is probably going to be hit by this bomb. Maybe we can stop that by destroying it or shooting down the plane carrying it, but we need the bomb. We need to take it apart and see inside. The Germans might take six months or more to build another one, but if we don't have it first, we're lost."

The wire fuse was a simple matter. The copper wire had to be removed from the bomb and pulled out of its sheathing. A low melting point lead and tin alloy wire then had to be inserted into the sheathing and replaced in the German bomb. This was a relatively simple but quite dangerous job for their spy.

When they next met with Vadim he was ecstatic. He had conveyed the instructions to his spy and the wire had already been replaced. Their resourceful cleaning lady had removed the required wire from a telephone set and inserted it in the sheathing.

Morris asked, "Vadim, how sure are you that it was done properly?"

"I am assured that it meets all the requirements you provided us with and that she has done what she says. Unfortunately we cannot bring her home as that would cause suspicion."

"We owe this woman quite a lot. Is there anything we can do for her?"

"We have assured her that her child will be well cared for."

Morris had learned not to pursue such statements so said nothing. But Vadim apparently needed to. "She had an accident on her way home from work. It was still dark and she stepped in front of an army truck leaving the laboratory."

"So she's gone?"

"Yes. A most courageous sacrifice. Unfortunately her children will... her child will never know of his mother's bravery."

Later that morning Morris, Willie, and George met with the PM at his underground headquarters near Whitehall. George, the only one of them privy to the location, received special permission to bring the two Americans with him. Although it was well past ten A.M., Churchill was in his dressing gown, sitting up on his bed.

"You're here with a most appalling report. We are to trust the Red's intent and believe this man Vadim? If you're wrong the consequences, as you are aware—"

George, totally out of character, interrupted his prime minister. "Sir, there is no alternative, there is no time. I believe you should leave London, as should the royal family."

"I will advise the king and it will be his decision. As for myself, we will remain in London to see through the outcome of this unfortunate situation."

"Sir, we must insist that you—"

"I am your prime minister, thus only Mrs. Churchill can insist. I would not order you to leave London as I know you would disobey, so now we're on this ship together. We must order air defense command to stand down when the airplane is spotted over the channel, and I must go to the palace, without raising suspicions, and inform the king."

Each evening Morris, George, Mary, and Max gathered at Admiralty House waiting for news that a lone plane had been spotted over the channel.

LONDON
SEPTEMBER 26, 1943

When word finally came they were joined by the PM and his bodyguards on the roof. As they looked toward Europe, standing apart from each other, each in their own thoughts, wondering what the next moments would bring, the unfamiliar distant sound of a jet engine grew in intensity. Mary, George, and Morris moved close together, bodies touching. The PM stood alone at the rail and relit his cigar. Max, who had already established a profound dislike for Churchill, emitted a low growl and leaned against Mary as if to protect her. Then they could see the red flame of its two engines, then the plane itself caught in the triangulation of antiaircraft spotlights. But no gunfire was heard and no tracer rounds were to be seen.

Mesmerized, they watched the plane release its dreadful cargo and arc upwards. Silence, no explosion, no flash of light; just calm, as if nothing had happened.

When they reached the bomb site just behind the palace, the special RAF team was already in place with American trucks and personnel surrounding the area. Willie, in uniform with no rank on his shoulders, was directing the operation. The bomb, as predicted, had survived its drop with only minor damage to its tail fins. It had half buried itself just inside the palace wall.

The RAF specialists in their pale blue uniforms were calmly squatting around the device and gently moving earth off the metal surface. One officer was holding a machine called a Geiger-Muller tube, which he passed back and forth over the bomb, and an elderly gentleman wearing a tweed jacket sat on the bomb itself. He was calmly using a rubber-coated wrench to unbolt an access plate near the broken tail fin. As the plate was slightly lifted the silence was broken by rapid clicking from the Geiger-Muller and a billow of acrid smelling smoke came pouring out. After a quick shrug at the others the man on the bomb carefully slid his fingers around the edges of the plate, and finding no trip wire or booby trap, lifted it up, quickly removed a smoldering silk bag, threw it over the wall, and then removed the three other bags and quickly replaced the access plate.

The clicking sound slowed and then stopped, but the smell remained. As the smoke cleared only a few participants and observers understood the devastation that had just been prevented. Willie slowly walked to a black car with a different smoke pouring from its open window, leaned over, and whispered, "All clear."

"Gather your cohorts and follow me to Number Ten. We could all use a drink."

"As much as I would enjoy that, Prime Minister, our work here is not completed."

Willie stood back and gave a sharp salute, which Churchill barely acknowledged with a wave of his cigar. Then turning to his driver said, "Take us home to Number Ten, Miss McKay."

George and Willie had established a team of RAF and U.S. Marines to remove the bomb. To any observer or the press, it was just another disarmed dud being taken for disposal, with the only newsworthy part being that it landed near the palace while the king and queen were in residence. This had happened several times during the past four years, with some bombs actually exploding, so this dud, although not that remarkable, might still be newsworthy.

The removal was straightforward. A short crane lifted the bomb on canvas slings into the bed of an open truck filled with sand. More sand was then shoveled on top to completely cover the cargo and a canvas tarpaulin was secured on top. Painted on the side of the truck was "Wainwright, Sherman & Davidson Coal, Ltd."

"It's a pity Mary couldn't squeeze in with us but it might draw attention, a beautiful young woman in the cab of a coal truck with three old men. I learned to drive these trucks in the first great war," Willie said to his two companions while grinding through the gears.

"Hitler must be apoplectic. Oh, to be a fly on the wall when the generals told him. This was his great secret weapon. The bomb to win the war and we stole it. We actually stole it! I will always be amazed that we pulled it off," Morris said with a laugh.

"Not so fast, my boy, your pal here is shredding the gears and we may never make it to the port."

"Don't worry. If I have to push this monster I will. I want it out to sea and away from population as soon as possible. Only then will we join Mary and that snobbish dog of yours and you'll open the best bottle you can find."

"Max doesn't dislike you, he just doesn't understand your—"

"Willie, turn left here. The road ahead is blocked."

"I have great respect for Max. He growls back at the PM."

"Make the next right turn and we're almost there."

When they arrived at the dock, the troop ship *Francis Y. Slanger* was waiting with steam up. Willie stopped on the quay and the three men jumped to the ground. The team of RAF and U.S. Marines were ready with slings and the truck was lowered into the aft hold. Within moments they all stood and watched as the ship slipped her lines and was towed out to sea for her Atlantic crossing.

George finally interrupted their silence. "Let's go home and have that drink."

"You might have noticed that our vehicle is on that ship," Morris said, pointing to the *Francis Y. Slanger* disappearing in the distance.

"And you might have noticed that I am air vice-marshal and most of these men are wearing RAF blue. Sergeant, fetch the key for that lorry if you will."

"Let me locate a driver, sir?"

George smiled, and looking at Willie said, "That

won't be necessary, just the key, we have our driver with us."

When they finally reached the townhouse the lorry, now almost stripped of gears, rolled to a stop. Mary and Max were on the front step waiting and when she saw the expression on their faces she sat down as if totally drained. Max on the other hand bounded over to George and then Morris with welcoming enthusiasm as only a dog can. Turning to Willie he emitted a low growl.

"Max, don't you think it's time to forgive me for whatever I've done to offend you?" Willie asked, backing away. With that Max gave a last growl and returned to Mary's side. Mary got up and walked over to Morris. Putting her arms around him she whispered, "I didn't want to die without you and I don't want to live without you."

"Amazingly, my darling, after months of missteps, all went as planned. We are safe, London is safe, and the next step is up to the Navy."

"Not to spoil the moment for you two, but I really need that drink," Willie said, edging around Max.

The following day the "gang," now of four, heard from Vadim in a most unusual way.

A delivery of flowers addressed to Mary arrived at the townhouse. The note attached read, "Congratulations. I am afraid I will be unable to attend your wedding celebration because I must return to my homeland. May you dance all night until the golden sunrise.

These flowers are from our garden. With much affection. Tommy."

"Why is it signed Tommy?" Mary asked, passing the note to Morris.

"Vadim must be under close surveillance, be in some sort of trouble and expects the note to be read by his minders. George, can you make anything of it?"

George studied the note carefully and then looked at the flowers.

"These look almost funereal; not what one would expect. He is telling us something. And the poetic line about golden sunrise is not—"

"I believe I understand it," Mary interrupted. It's Golders Green Crematorium."

"Yes, of course," George added. "Pavlova's ashes. Pavlova the Russian dancer, may you dance all night, golden sunrise. Golders Green at dawn."

"We should all go. I can pose as an admirer of Anna Pavlova and leave the flowers outside the gate. The three of you can look for Vadim. I believe we owe him our help."

"Let's come prepared: a large automobile and side arms," Willie added.

Morris started to say something. "I don't think Mary—"

"Don't you dare finish that sentence," she snapped at him. "If you're so worried, Max will be my protector."

By early morning they had decided to be conspicuous. Willie arrived in the ambassador's Cadillac flying an American flag, followed by a Ford sedan with two well-armed Marines. If Vadim wanted to defect, they would make it happen.

It was not yet dawn when they arrived. Mary went to the gate and stopped. She stood still, holding the flowers and looking down at Vadim, who had a small bullet hole in his forehead. Morris, seeing her drop the flowers and step back, came rushing over. Willie signaled to the Marines, who jumped out of the Ford with weapons drawn and scanned the road. George, seeing his daughter was safe, ran across the road to get a broader view. Max, who had followed him, sensed some movement behind a parked car and advanced in a crouch. George gave the command "GO," and Max's 120 pounds was on the man before he could react. The screams in Russian and English were frightening. George ran over with his gun drawn and seeing the man's bloody arm trying to protect his throat, called Max off. The dog seemed to be taking an extra few moments to back off, so George repeated the command. "MAX OFF."

The Russian looked up at him with relief and tried to get on his knees, but Max would have no part of it. He growled and the man slumped back down. "Net sobaki, no more dog, net sobaki."

By this time Morris and Mary had come over and Willie, with his two Marines, was standing perimeter guard.

"Are you alright, Daddy? Vadim is dead."

"I thought as much. Max was quite amazing, fearless. We may just have the killer in front of us."

Still on the ground, the Russian was holding his bloody arm and trying not to look at Max, who was eyeing him as prey.

George called over to Willie, "Let's get this fellow in the car, take him home, and feed him to the dogs."

"No, nyet, nyet, no dogs."

"Well now we know he understands English."

After the Russian was loaded into the Ford and driven away, the "gang of four" walked over to the gate, George bent to close Vadim's eyes, Mary picked up the flowers and placed them on his chest, and the four stepped back in silence for a long moment.

"Are we leaving him here?" Mary asked.

"I think we have to," Willie answered. "He'll be found soon enough and hopefully treated with respect. We just can't acknowledge our connection and put more people at risk. I believe he was killed because his job was done, that he was killed by his own people to ensure his silence. It may be time for the four of us to leave London for a while."

"I can arrange with RAF transport command today and we can be in the States by tomorrow night. Better not to be available for questions from our own people when they find Vadim. Too many people know a little about us and something will eventually be revealed."

"Daddy, I thought I would have to argue with you

to get you to leave London."

"I'm looking forward to time with David, my new grandson."

"What about our Russian prisoner?"

"Well, my dear," Willie answered, "he will not survive his wounds."

"But he only—" Mary interrupted herself, "Oh, I see."

They drove directly to the U.S. embassy, where George arranged the flight to Montreal, with a refueling stop in Gander, for that afternoon. George, Morris, and Mary went to the townhouse to pack and Willie contacted his agents in the States to arrange transport to New York, and to check on the progress of the *Francis Y. Slanger*, which he knew was soon to be disguised as a hospital ship and diverted to the Panama canal.

The flight to America was uneventful for most. The other passengers were RAF ferry pilots returning to pick up their next delivery of Canadian and U.S.-made airplanes. Most were asleep for much of the flight. Willie however, was not quite so comfortable as Max spent the flight lying on the cabin floor between George and Mary, watching him. Whenever he moved Max would open his eyes and stare. Finally he asked George. "I just don't understand, I like dogs, some of my best friends have dogs."

"He was like that with Morris until he married into the family. I'm sorry to say Mary is my only daughter. Just accept him."

NEW YORK CITY
SEPTEMBER 28, 1943

When they finally landed in New York after changing
planes in Montreal, George and Mary cleared immigration with diplomatic status, and Max was granted
the same. Apparently Willie had arranged all this in
advance. A large Packard was waiting on the tarmac
to take them to the Riverside Drive apartment, and
Willie left in a separate car to meet his people downtown. When they got in the car a small package was
waiting for each of them. "Mr. Sherman told me not to
leave until you opened them," the driver said without
getting in the car.

George received a Webley Revolver, Morris a Colt
.45 automatic, and Mary an Italian Beretta. Each came
with a box of ammunition, a holster, and a permit from
the War Department.

Morris, examining the permit said, "Willie is a cau-
tious man and after Vadim's murder I appreciate the
gift." The last package, addressed to Max, contained
an obvious bribe: a leather collar embossed with the
RAF symbol, and a New York State dog license.

"He also never gives up," George added, putting
the new collar on Max.

When they arrived at the apartment no one was
there to greet them. Morris, not having his key, tried

to convince a new doorman that he was in fact David's father. Mary had more success, explaining that she was his stepmother and that the distinguished man with the dog was his grandfather and that, due to the war, they had not seen each other for over a year.

As they crowded into the elevator David came rushing in the building yelling, "Wait for me." Out of breath, he explained that he had seen their car pass him on Broadway and had run the eleven blocks home. "I told grandma I would meet her at home and not to run." With that said, to Morris' amusement he pushed his way in and gave Mary an enormous hug. Then turning to his father, he said, "I really missed you," and hesitantly at first, hugged him too. Then he put his hand out to shake George's but was undone by being wrapped in George's arms. "I'm so glad to see you, David. We have all missed you terribly." Seeing all this, Max finally lost his self-control and in a rarely seen gesture jumped up and put his front paws on David's shoulders, almost knocking him over.

"Let me introduce you two. David, this is Max of the RAF, and Max, this is my grandson, David." Max actually licked David's face, something he had never been seen to do before, and then regaining his composure, sat down.

"My god, David, you're as tall as I am!" Mary said.

Blushing, David replied, "I noticed that when I hugged you."

"Can we go up now?" the elevator man asked. It

was only then that they realized the elevator buzzer was being repeatedly rung. On the way up the operator called out to the waiting tenants, "Right back four, right back seven, right back eleven." When they finally reached the twelfth floor and disembarked, the operator said, "Welcome back, Mr. Gold, we all missed you."

"Thank you, Andy, it's good to be home.

NEW YORK CITY
1945

Life did not exactly return to normal in the Gold household. David, who was now fifteen, traveled the city on his own, and now that others were around he no longer felt obligated to help his grandmother with the shopping. George had moved into an apartment on Broadway and Eighty-sixth Street, used as a safe house by his government. It was under surveillance by the FBI, MI5, and maybe the Germans and the Russians as well. There were no safe secrets in the dark world. He had dinner with Morris and his family often and made frequent trips to Washington, flying himself from Floyd Bennett Field certifying aircraft for delivery to the RAF. His function of record was coordinating armaments between the U.S. Army Air Corps and the Royal Air Force. In actuality, those with knowledge of the bomb theft were being protected from kidnapping or assassination by Willie's team of U.S. Marines and RAF special units.

After a time life became more normal. The German bomb was delivered to Tinian in the Mariana Islands, and the job of the "gang of four" seemed completed.

In Los Alamos, construction of two bombs was almost completed. The redesign of the fuse for the first bomb based on the stolen German bomb was in place and the plutonium bomb was in its final assembly stage. It was decided that the American uranium bomb would be used for the final test and the German bomb used operationally. There was less confidence in the plutonium bomb, called Fat Boy. It would be used, if necessary, several days after the uranium bomb.

Shortly after New Year's Morris was summoned and met with the president at his home in Hyde Park, New York. It was a pleasant enough drive for a while with light snow and temperatures in the low twenties. Tom Quinn had been sent to pick Morris up and the conversation ranged from the best delicatessen in New York, a subject on which they adamantly disagreed, to David's progress in school, and baseball. Then, after a long uncharacteristic silence, Tom said, "I'm worried. I think the boss is failing. The other day I don't think he could remember his doctor's name. He covered it up by calling him Doc. Not something he would normally do. He just seems so old and tired."

"Well, Tom, this happens when elderly people get tired. The strain of this war—"

"I understand that. I just can't accept it happening to him. What will we do? Mr. Truman is no FDR."

Having no answer, Morris was silent, and wanting to change the subject he asked, "Do you really believe the Stage Delicatessen is better than Barney Greengrass?"

Tom didn't answer, choosing to concentrate on his driving and his worries.

When Morris was led in the president was in a large upholstered armchair, wrapped in an afghan.

"Mo, I'm glad you could visit. That was quite a show you fellows put on in London. Even Winston had high praise for you and I think he has finally forgiven you for your Hess shenanigans."

Morris was shocked by the president's appearance and demeanor. His speech was slow and his light-hearted comments seemed strained. He looked small and frail. Tom had been right; he appeared to be failing quickly.

"I need you and... Sherman to join me on my trip to Yalta the end of the month. I think it would be helpful if that RAF fellow, your father-in-law, came along with us as well."

It was clear to Morris that the president couldn't recall Willie or George's full names and that he knowingly would need help dealing with Stalin and Churchill at the conference.

"Of course. I'll work out all the details with General Watson and we'll be there."

The president brightened, and with full clarity said, "Mo, we must honor our agreements but not give Stalin any more than we must. Churchill would renege on everything if he could get away with it. But he knows he cannot. He could never be forgiven. We are in a stalemate of our own making. Winston can't reveal that he authorized this bomb being dropped on London, Uncle Joe can't reveal that he let us steal the bomb, and I can't reveal that we let Russian agents share our atomic secrets. As a dictator, Stalin has the least to lose. He can eliminate his adversaries.

"This will be a difficult time, giving up a part of Europe that we liberated, sharing a divided Germany, and holding a line in northern Japan. I'm not thinking you boys did wrong, you did what you had to, just that it's a hell of a price to pay."

The president, obviously exhausted, then closed his eyes and fell asleep.

On the drive home Morris and Tom spoke in whispered tones. Tom adored the president and could not imagine his failing and Morris, shocked by FDR's condition, suggested that they should prepare themselves for what might become a slow deterioration. Tom explained that he had faced this with his own father and knew what to expect.

"But my dad only had five children. The boss has millions."

Passing Ninety-sixth Street it was agreed they should stop at Barney Greengrass, ten blocks away, and pick up some of the president's favorite foods for Tom to take back with him. After shopping the two men solemnly shook hands and parted, Morris walking the few blocks to his home and Tom driving the ninety miles north to Hyde Park.

On January 23, Morris, Willie, and George joined the president at Newport News, Virginia, and sailed with him aboard the heavy cruiser USS *Quincy*, arriving in Yalta on the second of February. They met with Churchill and his collection of aides and advisors and then flew to the Crimea for the conference with Stalin and his players.

The meetings began on a cooperative note. All three leaders wanted the unconditional, total surrender of Germany. The more difficult issues had to do with the divided administration of a postwar Germany and the establishment of Polish borders.

FDR called on Stalin to open a new front against Japan. He agreed under the condition that the Mongolian Republic remain untouched and that the Soviet Union regain its territory lost to Japan in 1904. For Willie this seemed a misguided and totally unnecessary compromise as he was sure the bomb, once demonstrated, would quickly end the war with Japan. But the president insisted he had negotiated a good compromise with Stalin. It appeared to many that Stalin had taken advantage of the president's weakened capabilities and actually seized control of the conference. Churchill, in private meeting with the Americans, insisted that Stalin was not to be trusted and that even these new borders would never be honored.

"That monster will invade Poland and all of eastern Europe as soon as the war with Germany is over. There will be no end to hostilities. History will remember this conference as a fool's errand." Morris and Willie flew home ahead of the president, who was meeting with the Saudi king, but George remained as an advisor to the highly disappointed and agitated prime minister.

During their absence from New York, Max had actually made a few friends in Riverside Park and Mary and David had resumed their riding. When the apartment next to them came available Sarah had rented it and put a connecting door between the two. This way she knew her family would stay close to her.

Life soon took on a real degree of normality. The war in Europe was obviously coming to a close with allied troops already inside Germany and several secret entreaties for conditional surrender being made by the German High Command.

One morning, while reading the *Times*, David said, "Dad, do you have any respect for all these countries declaring war on Germany now that it's almost defeated. I mean look at this list. Paraguay, Peru, Venezuela, Turkey, and Syria. All this month. Where were they when it took courage?"

"That's just it, David. Courage is a very special attribute, not to be confused with human nature, not to be expected, but to be honored when it exists. I don't know if courage is a natural part of our human makeup. It may be a very difficult choice and not second nature to us. Think of all the Germans who did nothing to stop Hitler. Do you believe they all agreed with him? Are they all cowards?"

"It's more confusing to me than that, Dad. Why did those Jews just go to the camps, why didn't they fight?

Now people are saying how terrible it is, but we knew, we talked about it in school. Why didn't the president do anything about it? It's not just the Germans, it's almost everyone."

"Maybe we should think of human character as a continuum that we all move along. Sometimes in fear, sometimes with courage, but mostly unchallenged by either."

Mary, who had seemed not to be paying attention, looked up from her crossword and said, "Few, but enough to matter, live at the courageous extreme."

Morris got up, kissed Mary, and gave David an affectionate pat. "I'm headed to my office. Don't forget that Grandpa George is arriving tonight."

Both Mary and David looked at him as if he were an idiot.

"Did you really think we might?" David asked.

"Just go to work, dear. Dinner is at six-thirty. Sarah is trying a kosher style haggis for my father. She says it's really similar to something called stuffed kishka."

"God help us."

Morris had reopened his Fifth Avenue office overlooking the skating rink, and once again began his practice of the law. Some clients returned, but for the most part his work consisted of referrals from Jimmy Roosevelt and Jimmy's mother, the first lady.

When Morris arrived home that night, David and his grandmother were ganging up on Mary in a game of hearts.

"This is really unfair," Mary grumbled.

"Looks like Mary is trying to shoot the moon," David said.

"Yes, one of us has to try and take a heart."

"See what I mean. Totally unfair."

"That's why I never play games with those two. They're merciless."

"That's not really true, Dad, you just don't like losing to greater minds."

"You and your grandmother are card sharps. I'm glad to see that you treat Mary as unfairly as you do me. Where's George?"

"Father took Max to the park and should be back very soon."

Sarah looked up and said, "I thought it would be a nice treat to go out for dinner tonight."

Morris looked at David and Mary and saw the almost imperceptible negative nod and knew not to ask about the Jewish style haggis.

"We thought the Tip Toe Inn."

"Good choice. Something for everyone."

It was a family restaurant on Broadway and Eighty-sixth Street, just a few blocks from their home. The waiters were a little gruff, but the food was always excellent. It was clearly Sarah's table, as so many of the other diners seemed to know her. They each had different dishes and passed their plates around to share. This was still a new, but enjoyable, experience for Mary and her father; the openness of their new family was a delight to both of them.

"Morris, without turning, the two men sitting at three o'clock look quite out of place," George said softly. "Look at their shoes."

"OK. When we leave let's move quickly so we have a good head start. The three of you turn toward home on Eighty-sixth Street and walk fast but don't run. George and I will duck into the entrance of Two-Fifty-Seven and try to get behind them. Of course they may just be having dinner and not out to follow us. In that case we'll see you at home."

"You'll see us at home in either case," Mary said firmly, while slipping her purse onto her lap and transferring the Beretta to her coat pocket.

"Of course. It just might take a little longer. Don't worry."

Morris put down more than enough money to cover dinner and tip and said, "Let's go."

The five got up and quickly walked out of the restaurant. Passing the cashier, Sarah said, "It's on the table. We have to run."

The five of them moved fast, and as planned Morris and George ducked into the entranceway of 257. Morris flashed his government ID to the doorman and put his finger to his lips. By the time the two men from the restaurant rounded the corner Mary, Sarah, and David were well down the block, almost at West End Avenue. As the men approached, George stepped out in front of them, gun in hand, and smiled. Both men froze. Before they could react Morris came up behind them and in a soft voice said, "Ruki vverkh." Russian for hands up.

After a second Morris, still in a soft voice said, "Now, or die on the street." Both men complied and were pushed out of sight into the entranceway and searched.

"Looks like we have a couple of diplomats," George said, after removing their weapons and checking their documents.

"We have immunity. You must release us at once."

Morris laughed. "We're private citizens stopping a robbery. Your immunity means nothing to us."

"What do you want of us?" the larger of the two men asked.

"I think that question belongs to us."

"George, hold these two gangsters here while I use the telephone inside. If they move, shoot them in the spine."

It took about ten minutes for Willie's men to arrive and take Boris and Boris away.

At the apartment everything was in order. Sarah had made tea and heated up the apple strudel she had planned for dessert.

After retelling the events Sarah asked, "Morris, how did you know the Russian for hands up?"

"My babushka would say 'ruki vverkh' to make sure our hands were clean before dinner. I also know 'vytri nogi,' but I didn't think that would work."

"What's that mean, Dad?"

"Wipe your feet."

The next morning Willie called to say that the Russians had agreed to leave the Gold and Wainwright family alone.

"How did you manage that, my friend?"

"I agreed not to execute their scientists who are at Los Alamos."

"And our two Russians?"

"Being held as future currency, small change but still valuable."

A few weeks later, Morris received the telephone call he had been expecting. It was from a sobbing Tom Quinn to say the president was dead. Apparently a massive stroke had taken him and there had been nothing that could have been done to save him. Tom had been right. The president had millions of children, all of whom were heartbroken and feeling lost. For those old enough he had taken them out of the Great Depression, and for those younger he was the only president they had known. He had brought them all through a world war. For the Golds it was additionally a more personal tragedy.

The following week, Morris and Mary had dinner with Jimmy Roosevelt in a private room at the Harvard Club. The two men reminisced about the pranks that had involved the president and how much he had loved gossip about their contemporaries, and the terrible food and drink they had shared together.

"I don't think this country will ever see anyone

close to him. He will be mourned during any presidency that does not live up to his standard. And that will be most. Here's to the boss."

With that, Morris and Jimmy parted for the evening, wondering if their relationship would ever be the same.

Whereas Willie remained with his job but now as part of the Truman administration, Morris no longer had any connection. It became clear that the new president knew nothing of the "gang of four," or for that matter the Manhattan Project. Not being respected or trusted by Roosevelt and his cronies, he had been kept in the dark about most everything. This, president Truman and his associates rightfully resented.

Truman's first meeting with General Groves was a shock. Both the almost unbelievable power of the bomb and the tremendous expense without congressional approval. He was sure laws had been broken but also knew that this was no time to besmirch Roosevelt's reputation. The war was almost over and he had no political power, only his predecessor's reputation to follow. Truman was viewed as a lame duck from the moment of his swearing in. He was a nobody and president of the United States at the same time. His election in three years was seen as unlikely. Groves, having become a Roosevelt insider, decided that it was unwise and unnecessary to trust the new president with how the uranium bomb had been acquired and the great price paid to the Soviets.

He had no doubt, and easily convinced Truman, that after the German surrender the country had but one goal. Getting out of war. If we had a way to quicken that end we should use it. The bombs were ready and all the talk of a demonstration on some underpopulated Pacific island was pacifistic and weak. The Japanese had to suffer a horrendous defeat before they would surrender. Also, as Truman put it, "If any doubt remains that we are the most powerful nation on Earth, this will convince them otherwise." He, of course, had no knowledge of what the Soviet's knew. All hope in the Los Alamos community that the bomb would be a deterrent, rather than a weapon of mass destruction, was lost. Any decent man was viewed as treasonable and you lost your security clearance and might, if viewed as a risk, be detained.

On August seventh, Morris, George, and Mary saw the terrifying result of their efforts. The *Times* article said that the city of Hiroshima on the Japanese mainland had been so obliterated by a cloud of dust and smoke that no accurate damage assessment could be made. The power of the bomb was given as 2,000 times that of any previous bomb.

"We are responsible for this," Morris said. "It was our bomb, the German bomb. We know that the city was probably destroyed, how many people must have died. What happened to the demonstration bomb?"

"Is this Truman fellow following President Roosevelt's plan, or did he make this decision on his own?"

George asked. "He's threatening 'a rain of ruin' for Japan. That seems to indicate the other bomb will probably be used."

"He's the president now and he could have stopped it. I think we should have known that if politicians had these bombs they would use them."

It was Mary who spoke next. "Morris, my dear, I think we always really knew that to be true. The alternative of the German politicians having them was unthinkable. That is why we did what we did. And we are responsible."

"I know, darling, and someday I will have to tell David and hope he will understand."

CODA

RIVERSIDE DRIVE
NEW YORK CITY
NOVEMBER 27, 1970

My father did finally tell me. Posthumously. It took
two years for me to finally start going through his
papers. I did this more as a voyage through my undefined grief than as a mission of duty. In this archive of
over fifty years of my father's law practice, I was hoping to find some genuine individuality for myself and
a detachment from or dissolution of that encumbering
part of me that was my father. Anything to show that
he was a normal being rather than the perfect example
of integrity and honesty that I had spent so much of
myself trying to emulate. It has been said that the last
great gift a father can give his son is his death. Well,
if that is the case, I was having trouble unwrapping it.
Like a four-year-old trying to tear open his birthday
present the joy of the moment eluded me. Even now, in
my forties, I could not feel his equal. It had something
to do with being Jewish. I had been brought up to
believe that Jews are obligated to commit themselves

to a path of righteousness through helping others. My father seemed the high priest of this commitment. I was looking for the flaw in his character. The mortal trait, the sign of weakness that would allow me to love his memory and perhaps feel equal to the man. I do not consider myself particularly good or ethical. Without question, I have helped others without gain to myself, but I have also knowingly done harm to others for my own benefit.

I resisted the belief that my father had been any different. Without the slip or flaw I was looking for, I would spend the rest of my life feeling inferior to and resentful of him. I worked my way through the wall of old file cabinets in the basement of my father's brownstone on Riverside Drive. This building, now mine, had been his office and, for the last twenty years, his home. This monument, which had been visited by great men of finance, business, and politics was for me a monument to my frustration and failed impersonation. Even this sectioned storage area of the basement, with its old but meticulously stacked cabinets, was filled with the perfection of his life. Every moment of Morris Gold's law practice was consecutively numbered and cross-referenced with an alphabetical card index.

I remembered when my father came to see my first office. We had planned on having lunch together at the dairy restaurant on Forty-seventh Street. My father almost never went out to lunch and I knew that he would have preferred his Swiss cheese and tomato on rye in his own conference room rather than in a crowded restaurant, but this day was to be special; it was to be about me. I was proud of my new office and wanted my father to see it and, hopefully, approve of it. I was afraid this would be a black or white lesson in right and wrong as judged by Morris Gold. The first thing he did was pull open my top file drawer with its small group of files arranged just as his were but, instead of starting with the number 1, my first case was numbered 1001. As much as I have tried I have never released myself from my guilt.

I wrongfully dreaded something like, "Do you think your clients will think you're a big shot with over a thousand cases under your belt? You're only twenty-eight years old. An honest lawyer doesn't have to fool his clients and an honest man doesn't try." But instead he said, "I should have done that numbering when I started my practice, much easier to keep track of files that way." This was the first time as an adult that I had exposed my work to my father for approval. We did have our lunch out but it was a sullen occasion for me. I was ashamed of myself for harboring such a childish fear of disapproval from a man who had done everything he could to be a loving father. To this day I don't know if my father realized my need for his approval and if he did how much it troubled him.

I started my search with his diaries. These were meticulous notes on all of his visitors and telephone calls. Each time something seemed promising, a cross check of the files would show it to be completely in keeping with his image, even the notation that had so raised my interest: "July 12, 1946—destroy notes from Mary Callahan and send additional $1,500." Mary Callahan, it turned out from checking the files, was a secretary at the archdiocese of New York and was using the money loaned by my father to rescue children from the DP camps in Europe. He had made the money a gift and added an additional gift of $1,500. The total had come to over $5,000, a substantial sum in the 1940s. Another Morris Gold good deed. He wasn't even selfish enough to restrict his aid to Jewish children. The money was used to bring Catholic and Protestant and even German children to the States. I had never heard about these gifts; my father rarely spoke about himself in specifics. But the message was always gotten across, be responsible for others as well as for yourself. I felt driven to continue the search. I still don't completely understand why, but the feeling was the same feeling I had had when, as a small boy, I had secretly looked through my father's top dresser drawer. Somehow both places—his file room and his top dresser drawer—held some mystical or magical fascination and danger. I felt as though these private places held the power to release me from my father's hold.

On the third day of looking, I found a diary notation for January 12, 1952: "Congressman Nixon, 3 P.M., Capital Airlines, Idlewild." It was really unbelievable. Morris Gold hated Richard Nixon and everything he represented. This hatred predated the entry in the diary, and really started in 1950 when Nixon had been so terribly devious in his campaign against Helen Gahagan Douglas. But what really made this entry so strange was that I had so often heard my father say he was sorry he had never met Nixon so he could have looked him in the eye. Nixon's name was not used lightly in the Gold household and the mere mention of it brought an unusually harsh comment from above.

"Harry Truman chose his words well: 'Nixon is a goddamned shifty eyed liar.'"

What was my father doing meeting Richard Nixon at Idlewild Airport and why was the meeting never mentioned in any of his anti-Nixon pronouncements? Somehow I knew I had found what my father used to call "the can of worms," and without question I was going to open it. It was an easy matter to look back in the diary, find the new cases or clients closest to January 12, 1952, check the alphabetical card index and find the file numbers. This done, I could simply pull the adjacent files and, hopefully, have some answers. But one of them, file #5210, was a dummy; it merely contained the overflow from the previous file. Both files together would not have filled a single file folder. Obviously my father had removed something, as the numbers on the folders were in his handwriting. Then I saw it and I knew. In the corner of the folder was written, as if a carelessly jotted note, 11W42. The address of my first office. Eleven West Forty-seventh Street. I checked the index cards for Eleven West Forty-seventh and pulled out the file. File number 1001. It was titled *Powers vs. Powers.*

That was my first case, the one I had numbered 1001. My father had coded this file in a way that only I would understand; it had to contain something he wanted only me to see. The thin file contained two sealed envelopes. The first had twenty-six receipts for annual payments on a safe deposit box at the Eighty-fourth Street branch of Chase Manhattan Bank and one receipt for $200 to be applied in the event of non-payment. At current rates, depending on the size of the box, this would cover five to ten years of rental. The box was listed in the name of Morris Gold or David Gold. Although I had no memory of ever signing an access card, I already knew where the key to the safe deposit box was. It was in a little carved wooden box in my father's top dresser drawer, the drawer that had so intrigued me as a child. I could picture every item in that box: my mother's and my grandparents' obituary notices from the *New York Times.* My grandfather's from before the infamous and what would have been to him shameful, name change from Goldstein to Gold. Also in the box was my mother's gold watch, a small glassine envelope with a lock of my grandmother's hair, a set of gold general's stars, and the until now unidentified key.

Then I opened an envelope I had never seen before, which was addressed to me.

My dearest David,

This journal will be a record of my actions immediately before, during, and after the war. You will wonder why I have never discussed this time of my life with you, you may even be quite angry with me for this, but I believe that after you have finished reading and have taken the time to reflect, you will accept my decision. Men complete great endeavors of which they are justifiably proud, and those of which they are equally ashamed. As I have never come to terms myself with my own participation, my own responsibility, for these events, I cannot predict how you will view my actions. But please, my dear son, understand that today, tonight, I am prostrate with shame and defeat.

I affirm to you that the deposition I am about to write is, to the best of my recollection, a true and faithful accounting of my participation in the events leading up to this darkest hour.

May their children forgive me.

Note: You will also find a packet of wartime letters between Mary and myself. Although somewhat explicit, I share them with you because I want you to understand the great love we had and continued to have for each other.

Your father,
Morris Goldstein
June 19, 1953

The journals he led me to are surprisingly candid and I considered leaving out some more personal parts and some parts that paint less than favorable pictures of people I respect. My father recorded his war in great detail for a reason and I believe his history needs to be told in its fullest. No truth too important to be redacted, no action too private to be hidden and no lie too secret not to be revealed. Some characters have been merged for clarity and some names have been altered for security reasons. The journals ended in 1945.

Max died in 1954, at the age of fifteen. Many friends, including Willie, who was then an advisor to President Eisenhower, attended the ceremony at Riverside Park. Back at the apartment George pulled Willie aside and said, "That dog had a great sense of humor and I believe he really enjoyed teasing you."

"I knew that, and I knew I could count on him as a friend."

David's grandmother remained the family matriarch until her passing at the age of eighty-seven.

After returning to England in 1956, George retired from the RAF, settled in the new State of Israel and became an advisor to their air force.

Morris and Mary remained in New York and bought a brownstone on Riverside Drive. She became active in the civil rights movement and in 1965 marched with Dr. King and thousands of others from Selma, Alabama, to the steps of the capitol in Montgomery. She developed the same coronary heart disease that had felled her mother and died the following year after completing the Sunday *Times* crossword puzzle, sitting in her favorite chair, looking over the Hudson River.

Morris practiced law until he no longer could, and in 1968, sitting in that same chair, took his own life using Mary's Italian Beretta.